"A magical, eye-opening read. The similarities and differences between two teenage girls—a Canadian and an African—are very revealing. I love that each girl has a taste of the other one's life and that they find a way of doing something constructive in their lives."

Aimee Webb
Grade 9, South Okanagan Secondary School, Oliver, BC

"A fast-paced and moving story filled with discovery, truth, and mystery. Riley sees and experiences change in a country entirely new and strange to her. Suspenseful and powerful, GABBRA'S SONG is a fascinating book!"

Sierra Komar
Grade 7, KVR Middle School, Penticton, BC

"GABBRA is a beautiful story – more than a treat. I absolutely loved it!"

Milly Bird
Penticton, BC

"This book was great – thrilling to the last. Young adults will read GABBRA'S SONG and enjoy it tremendously. My compliments to Jane Volden – she really made it work!"

Kirsten Lisa Schmid
Grade 8, Shuswap Middle School, Salmon Arm, BC

"Teenagers from completely diverse backgrounds meet, with narrowing eyes, to look at each other's lifestyles; their emotions; only to learn they are not so different after all. GABBRA'S SONG is a poignant story of intrigue that ends in tender young love under an African sun; a story that is important to young people growing up in a new world where, hopefully, the poison of old racial issues will be swept away in a new understanding and respect of whom we really are."

Rima Publications, **BC**

GABBRA'S SONG

by
JANEY M VOLDEN

Trafford Publishing
6E – 2333 Government Street
Victoria, BC V8T 4P4   Canada
www.trafford.com

Editing & Design: Gillian (Jill) Veitch. Kelowna, BC
Cover : Janey Volden & Jill Veitch
Photos: Janey Volden & Margaret Hayes
This book is typset in Garamond and Speedball.

www.janeyvolden.com

Note for Librarians: A cataloguing record for this book is available from Library and Archives Canada at www.collectionscanada.ca/amicus/index-e.html
ISBN 1-4251-0500-9

Printed in Victoria, BC, Canada. Printed on paper with minimum 30% recycled fibre.
Trafford's print shop runs on "green energy" from solar, wind and other environmentally-friendly power sources.

Offices in Canada, USA, Ireland and UK

Book sales for North America and international:
Trafford Publishing, 6E–2333 Government St.,
Victoria, BC V8T 4P4 CANADA
phone 250 383 6864 (toll-free 1 888 232 4444)
fax 250 383 6804; email to orders@trafford.com
Book sales in Europe:
Trafford Publishing (UK) Limited, 9 Park End Street, 2nd Floor
Oxford, UK OX1 1HH UNITED KINGDOM
phone +44 (0)1865 722 113 (local rate 0845 230 9601)
facsimile +44 (0)1865 722 868; info.uk@trafford.com
Order online at:
trafford.com/06-2258

10 9 8 7 6 5 4 3 2

To my late stepfather V.E.M. Burke
and my two sons Oliver and Casey

Acknowledgments

Grateful thanks to my first stepfather, the late Victor Burke, who gave me inspiration for GABBRA'S SONG while on safari to Northern Kenya in 1972.

To my second stepfather, the late Charles Hayes, Editor of the South Okanagan Review Newspaper, Okanagan Falls, BC: sincere appreciation for his encouragement to become a writer.

A million kudos to my mother, Margaret Hayes, my best friend and mentor, critique and guiding light. She encouraged me to keep a journal when I was a child and inspired me to observe the wonders of nature.

Warm hugs for my sisters Judi Roselli-Cecconi, Caroline Webb, and Christine Rougier-Chapman for their support and interest in the manuscript; to my brother and herpetologist Jules Sylvester for his invaluable knowledge on reptiles and bugs, and younger brother Roger Sylvester, for his unending sense of humour.

Special thanks and love to my husband Bruce Volden for his understanding, support and devotion over the years as GABBRA'S SONG became a reality.

To my close friends and the rest of my wonderful extended family all over the world: thanks for your continued enthusiasm.

Gratitude and deep appreciation to my editor, Jill Veitch, for her encouragement and support in revising the manuscript. *Asante sana, rafiki yango!* Thank you, my friend!

And finally, praise to my late husband Basil Bell, whose enthusiasm for adventure and wild safaris contributed to the spirit of Gabbra's Song.

Janey Volden
Okanagan Falls, British Columbia

Introduction

At the age of nine, Janey (Sylvester) Volden, left England, the country of her birth, to travel with her family to live in Kenya, East Africa.

Over the next 25 years, Janey and her brothers and sisters, Julian, Roger, Judith and Caroline traveled on many safaris where they learned to appreciate the vastness and beauty of Africa and its peoples.

On one of her last African safaris, Janey, accompanied by friends and her then stepfather, Victor Burke, traveled in a LandRover convoy over one thousand miles through the Northern Frontier District to Ethiopia; an extremely dangerous journey because of raiding *Shifta* (bandits) hiding out at that time in remote areas.

It was on this visit that she visited Dumbuluk* spring-water well where she met several young adults of the Borana tribe. Janey was inspired to write a novel from her diary notes made while in the Dida Galgalu desert.

During her schooling in East Africa and later working with the Food & Agriculture Organization/United Nations Development Programme (FAO/UNDP), Janey had the opportunity to make friends with people from all nations.

By 1980, Janey married hydrologist Basil Bell, but was sadly widowed when their son, Oliver, was a few months old.

Emigrating to British Columbia, Canada, Janey joined her mother Margaret and stepfather Charles Hayes as a partner in publishing the South Okanagan Review newspaper.

In 1982, Janey met Bruce Volden. They married in Penticton, BC one year later. Their son Casey Duff Volden was born in 1985.

Margaret Hayes
Okanagan Falls, British Columbia

---

* pronounced *doom*-boolook

Members of the Borana tribe meeting at a fresh water well.
(Pic courtesy of Department of Information, Kenya.)

Contents

Nomadic tribeswoman securing her child atop the family's
household belongings, ready to move to their next water hole.
(Pic courtesy of Department of Information, Kenya)

Prologue

GABBRA LED ME TO A HEAP of dead branches near the first camel-skin hut. "Riley, my friend, this is the secret safety tunnel where we will hide if the *Shifta* attack us," she whispered.

"You mean the Somali bandits your father talked about?" I asked, hardly daring to breathe.

She looked into the distance. "Yes. They raided our village several years ago."

Gabbra was silent for a moment. Then she continued. "A deep cave has been dug at the end of the tunnel—big enough to hold the children and our elderly people. One person pulls a thorny canopy over the top and we sit and wait quietly till the bandits have gone."

"That makes me feel nervous," I said, staring at her. "I wish you hadn't told me."

Gabbra said that in this time of extreme drought, the *Shifta* were probably desperate for water and camels. "We have to be prepared for an attack at any moment," she cautioned. "They will *never* have the chance to abduct our women again," she said fiercely.

I heard a pack of jackals yipping excitedly over their freshly killed prey just outside the protective thorn fence, and I shivered. "How will you know if they sneak in?"

Probably sensing my fear, Gabbra hugged me. "If it happens, I will run with you and the others to the tunnel. Our warriors watch for anyone suspicious travelling across the Plain of Darkness. My brother Nagya taught them a special warning signal that we're all familiar with."

Instantly my cheeks felt warm with thoughts of the handsome warrior for whom I had strong feelings.

"What signal?" I asked.

Instinctively, Gabbra pulled a shawl over her head and shoulders. "The song of a mourning dove."

Chapter 1

LAND OF SKELETONS

I PEERED THROUGH THE TINY WINDOW of the Cessna-172 piloted by my father. We were approaching Kenya's Northern Frontier District—a desert-like place in East Africa where years of drought had taken its toll. Scorched earth lay cracked and rippled. It looked like it hadn't rained in years.

The plane's low drone made me sleepy. I leaned back in my seat, listening to some new music on my MP3 player, and glanced over at Gabbra. My best friend was startlingly beautiful, with high cheekbones, intelligent dark eyes and generous lips. It was almost as though an artist had painted her a shiny milk-chocolate brown.

"Drought means death, doesn't it, Gabbra?" I said loudly over the roar of engines, but she didn't answer. Instead, tears slid slowly down her cheeks. I pulled the headphones from my ears, eased myself out of the seat and crouched down beside her. I'd never seen her cry before.

"Gabbra, what's wrong?" I asked, astonished. "Are you upset about those dead animals down there? Do you think your family has enough water? Are you crying because you…"

"Riley Jane Forbes," she said, smiling at me through her tears. "Will you please be quiet for once!" I wondered if she was emotional about seeing her father again. Gabbra wiped away tears with her slender brown fingers and smoothed out the creases in her long khaki skirt. "I told you before; only the fittest will survive because that has been our tradition for hundreds of years."

With a trembling finger, she pointed to the burnt earth below, "Look through my window. Isn't it wonderful?"

Leaning past Gabbra, I saw frightened gazelles scattering in every direction as the shadow of our plane darkened their eroded territory. Camels, looking like extra-terrestrial creatures, seemed to sway slowly across a land of craters and rocks. A dust-devil spiraled in the distance, reminding me of a galactic spacecraft, leaving moon dust in its wake.

She laid her hand on my arm. "I'm crying with happiness and pride because my brother Nagya has reached the important stage of manhood. I can't quite believe I'm coming home to see him after three amazing years with you in Canada."

My mind skipped back all those years ago when Dad and I first visited Dumbuluk. Gabbra's father—Chief Jallaba, leader of the Borana tribal community—had known Dad for many years. Perhaps that's why he entrusted his only daughter to come and live with us in British Columbia. He said it was an opportunity for her to have a proper education. Only *boys* were educated in their community; *girls* were forbidden to go to school and encouraged to marry by the age of fourteen.

When Gabbra was growing up, her brother Nagya had made an effort to teach her everything he learned from the local Catholic Mission School. Nagya and his father kept silent about her education to prevent her from being punished by the Borana Elders.

When she lived with us in Canada, Gabbra insisted on sleeping on the floor in my bedroom.

She ate plain rice and tofu, and buried her head in boring medical books every free moment.

Apart from our school uniform, Gabbra owned three white shirts and three long khaki skirts. She refused to wear jeans like the rest of us and for years I argued with her about her old-fashioned traditions. She had an answer to every one of my questions, but I could debate any subject to death. Why the heck didn't her family live beside the water well, I thought, squinting through the plane window again.

Gabbra's people were nomads. When the rains failed, her family would load their camels with entire huts made from sticks and skins, and travel from one water well to the next in search of fresh pasture. Sometimes they'd be forced to dig in the sand for water which lay just a few feet below the surface. She used to eat maggots and drink a mixture of camel's milk and blood. She said that's how nomads survived.

Thermal updrafts allowed vultures to circle at dizzying heights without even flapping their huge wings. Watching and waiting for something to die, these sinister shadows of doom soared above a graveyard of sun-bleached animal skulls and rib cages, pecked clean by frenzied scavengers.

Shuddering with the thought of dying from thirst, I rummaged in my backpack for a can of warm pop. An aromatic smell wafted out of the bag from a sweet melon I had brought with me.

Nagya.

Even hearing his name gave me a sharp thrill. I wondered if he would remember me from when Gabbra and I were giggling thirteen-year-olds. He seemed so mature at sixteen.

Although he had annoyed me from the moment I first met him all those years ago, there was also something mysterious about him. He had just returned from a thirty-kilometre trek by camel. I remember Nagya teased me about learning to do women's work like milking camels and building houses with mud and dung. Feeling insulted, I hurled harsh words at him. I said I was *never* going to milk a camel just because I was a girl. And forget about handling camel dung!

I grinned to myself as I caressed the clay camel necklace he had given me. That smelly, crudely-made thing had to be washed and sprayed with perfume every time I wore it.

"This camel is called *Ata Allah*," Nagya had said, smiling at me. "It means God's Gift. *Tutaonana,* white Riley-girl. In Swahili that means *we shall meet again.*" He had turned his back on me because he said it was bad luck to watch someone leaving on a long journey.

I had begged for Gabbra to come home with me. I whined so persistently that both fathers agreed.

Gabbra's father said, "My daughter can go, on condition she returns in three years for her brother's circumcision ceremony—it's the most important stage in a Borana man's life; it's when Nagya will become a warrior."

Circumcision? My father said I opened and closed my mouth like a goldfish gulping helplessly from the bottom of a dried-up pond.

Then Gabbra made a comment I would never forget. "If Father says I must, then I will go to school with Riley. But I promised something to my mother," she added firmly. "I swore to her I shall never lose my Borana culture."

"And what happens if you *don't* keep your promise?" I had asked her.

"To be killed by someone who loves me most will be my punishment if I break the oath," she replied softly, sending shivers all the way up the back of my neck.

Dad turned his head to talk to us. "Girls, stop shouting at each other back there. Riley, come up front and you can land this plane. Tell Gabbra to buckle up."

Once I was seated, Dad spoke to me through the headsets. "Riley, see that *manyatta?*" He pointed to a small village below surrounded by bushes. "Take her down and buzz the chief so he can meet us at the air strip with the LandRover. He'll need advance warning because it takes a little over an hour for him to drive there. We'll land and wait for him in the shade."

Taking the four-seater plane down to one thousand feet, we circled the *manyatta* and saw people building huts, camels plodding toward an enclosure of thorns and children waving their arms in the air. I remembered the times I sat between my father's knees when he taught me to fly. He called me "Little Red Fox" because of my small, wiry body, flaming red hair and sharp temper. I was strong-minded but I *did* learn how to maintain, fuel-up and pilot a small plane.

Dad was an agricultural consultant with the International Development & Disaster Agency (called IDDA), in Vancouver. It was an organization that sent consultants, emergency supplies and water pipelines to arid areas of Africa. He told me that he and Gabbra's father often worked together to form a liaison between the Kenyan Government, IDDA and the Borana community of northern Kenya.

I looked up at my father fondly, but my eyes also caught the familiar photo of Mom, still scotch-taped to the left of the pilot's seat. With a stab of sadness, I remembered listening to my parents arguing when I was eight years old. "Tom, I want to be on my own," my mother had said, admitting that she preferred to live on the dangerous and unpredictable edge as an international news reporter with a major news network. Before she left for her next assignment, she had hugged me. "Riley, you're so much like me—you will always be my feisty Irish pixie. You'll be a strong leader because people listen to you. It's important that you help change the world and make a difference. Be passionate about what you believe in."

Mom and I had a secret code that only the two of us understood. We linked the littlest fingers of our right hands together in solemn promise and exchanged a strand of red hair. She gave me her diamond nose stud and the last thing she said was, "Reach for the biggest and brightest star in the sky and your wish will come true."

That was the last time I saw my mother. She did not communicate with us very often on the internet and right now, Dad and I had no idea whether she was alive or dead in some war-torn country.

Pushing those thoughts away, I concentrated on heading the plane toward the rough airstrip. I had scrunched my hair into a long ponytail, shoving it through the back of a baseball cap I'd jammed on my head and, because it was hot, I wore my favourite tank top, cut-off jean shorts, and hightop sneakers.

Pulling back the throttle, I used the brake and steering pedals with my feet and landed the plane on a bushy air strip in the middle of nowhere. As I maneuvered around mounds of earth and rock, a frightened warthog snorted and bounded across the runway, its periscopic tail sticking straight up in the air. I flinched because the high bushes were so close that they scratched the struts of the plane. Finally, the slow *tic-tic-tic* of the propellers stopped. The cabin seemed airless and strangely silent after the plane's deafening roar.

"Excellent work, Riley," Dad said, patting my arm. "By the way," he looked disapprovingly at me, "I told you to wear something more respectable. Shorts are not appropriate where we are going." I ignored him and turned my head to the back of the plane, watching as Gabbra swung the tiny passenger door open. The little gold butterfly pendant necklace I'd given her shone and glittered in the fierce sun.

Dad went to hang the key off the oil dipstick under the engine cowling. It was a safety routine I learned when travelling with him. "It'll be safer here than in my pocket!" he laughed, reminding me of the time he'd washed his clothes in a fast-flowing river in Tanzania and both key and pants disappeared downstream.

My feet were sweaty inside those hightop runners. My throat was parched, and a haze of black sand flies irritated me. I watched as Gabbra shook her thickly braided hair from side to side to whisk the flies away from her face.

Dad put his arm around Gabbra's shoulders. "Your father is on his way. It's been a long time since you last saw him. You must be anxious to see him again," he said gently.

We sat under the shade of the plane's wing and waited for more than half an hour until we saw a cloud of dust snaking toward us. A tall, distinguished-looking man wearing a tan-coloured suit and safari hat stepped out of the LandRover and headed for the plane. He appeared the same age as Dad. Although a long scar disfigured his left cheek, his dark eyes gleamed like the black obsidian rock found around northern Kenya. He waved a fly-whisk which Gabbra said was made from giraffe hair, and held his other hand outstretched.

"It is good to see you *Bwana* Forbes," he said with a smile. "I trust your journey was good."

I glanced up from completing my flight plan journal and saw the Chief and Dad looking at me. Chief Jallaba chuckled and said, "I have to get used to a changing world with women doing men's work. Now where is my daughter?" I smiled at the Chief, expecting some acknowledgement, but he seemed to ignore me and walked toward Gabbra. Their greeting was respectful: a handshake at first, then alternate kissing of cheeks.

"We must drive to the *manyatta*," announced

the Chief. "The women are preparing food for us."

I stepped forward and put my hand lightly on the Chief's arm. "Do you not recognize me, Mr. Jallaba?"

Gabbra's father stared at me again, and then his gaze softened. "Riley! Of course! You were a young girl when I saw you last. Now you are a woman. I thank you for looking after my daughter and bringing her back to me," he said, and walked away. He swished the fly-whisk quickly through the air, as though dismissing me as a pest.

I stared at him. No handshake? No hug? I guess Gabbra and Nagya were right, I thought, women must stay in the background and keep quiet. Now I was annoyed. It's time to change things around here, I mused, kicking a lump of dry earth so viciously that a puff of fine powder exploded like a bomb. I jammed my hands into my shorts pockets. Good thing I wasn't staying in this desolate place. I consoled myself with the thought that I'd fly out with Dad the next day, and ran to the plane to get my backpack.

I had no idea that my life was about to turn upside-down in this strange African desert.

Northern Kenya is 'camel country':
An old LandRover is not the king of the road here!
(pics: Margaret Hayes)

Chapter 2

THE PLAIN OF DARKNESS

THE TRIP TO THE MANYATTA was not a comfortable drive down a little country road, nor was the land green and lush like the cattle ranches back home. This bumpy experience was like riding in a truck with square wheels. The heat was unbearable as we traveled through a shimmering savannah of thorn bushes and solitary trees. The LandRover seemed to split in half as it pitched and tilted, crawling slowly over a rugged, meandering track of grey sand, sun-baked boulders and pot-holes.

Dad had bought me an expensive camera and a stock of notebooks to record this spring break journey to Kenya.

He nudged my elbow, excitedly. "Quick Riley, take a picture of that weird-looking bird over there. *Bwana* Jallaba, would you stop for a moment?"

Dad told me that nobody had ever photographed the rare Streizman's Bush Crow successfully. "Get a few good shots, Riley. This is the only place in the world it lives. Maybe you can begin your next campaign and persuade the World Wildlife Society to hire you as a writer to research the species. By the way, it doesn't fly."

I leapt out. "Streizman" pounced onto a bundle of insects scuttling in the grass, but before it hopped away, I quickly adjusted the telephoto lens, auto-focused and clicked.

"Got it!" I exclaimed. My attempt at scrawling observation notes in my journal resulted in four almost unreadable words on each page. With difficulty, I hung on to the roll bar with one hand while clutching my camera with the other. Sometimes we'd be elevated to the roof, returning with a thump onto the metal seat.

I looked at Gabbra. She had closed her eyes, apparently oblivious to the twisting, bumpy track as we climbed forty-five degree hills and rumbled faster down the other side. Huge clumps of dung had been dumped down the narrow track— evidence of elephants in the area.

"Dried dung is good fuel for fires," said the Chief, as we travelled past an Acacia tree breaking under the strain of at least twenty staring baboons.

In the distance, high outcrops of land glared at us while mirages shimmered on the dead horizon. "We are in the middle of the barren Dida Galgalu Plain of Darkness," explained Gabbra's father. "We have another half hour before we reach the *manyatta* so I suggest we stop for tea."

Gabbra continued to stare blindly out the window. She had not said one word since we left the plane. Listening to crickets buzzing incessantly, I photographed the awkward beauty of dust-covered trees, cactus and poisonous desert roses. The Chief led us to the shade of an Acacia tree. He brought out a wooden *gourd* containing milky tea—refreshing and thirst-quenching. Just as the Chief was explaining that his tea container was a hollow dried-out pumpkin, I felt a tug on my arm. Gabbra pointed to a five-foot high termite hill.

"Thank you for finally resurfacing from the land of the dead!" I joked.

"Look carefully," she said, ignoring my

comment. "Do you see a long red snake lying on top of the ant hill?"

"Yes, yes. I hate snakes, but I see it. We should get back into the LandRover," I said, urgently.

"It's a spitting cobra. If we leave it alone it won't harm us. I know it's a red spitting cobra by the black ring around its throat. In the old days, women from quarrelling tribes would poison their enemies with snake venom."

I gaped at her.

"It did not happen very often," she continued, "but several years ago, if an oath or promise was broken, the Elders of the community—who took this very seriously—designated a young girl to fetch the venom. They kept it in a cool place inside the Head Elder's hut, and would mix it with camel's milk…"

"You mean they kept the snake in the hut?" I interrupted her.

"Wait, Riley, let me explain. I'll give you an example of what happens." Gabbra was always patient with me. "The Elders order a warrior to search for a spitting cobra. After whacking off the snake's head, the warrior squeezes the venom out into a small, narrow ivory or horn snuff container. The unsuspecting law-breaker is given the drink—crystallized venom stirred into camel's milk—and dies within hours. Even a mild dose of neurotoxin in the venom would bring on shallow breathing, slurred speech, muscle twitches and slight deafness. Then the victim finally passes out in a coma or dies, depending on how much poison is swallowed. It looks like a natural death, but in fact it's murder," she said.

"That's horrible!" I gasped.

"Well, in our tradition, we do not break the law," said Gabbra, solemnly.

Almost as though it was eavesdropping, a secretary bird, with its plumed head cocked jauntily to one side, strutted down the road on tiptoes, like the judge in a courtroom.

"Father, will you tell Riley and Mr. Forbes a little more about our Borana ancestry? I think they will be interested."

Chief Jallaba frowned, drank from the *gourd*, and wiped his mouth. "At the end of the nineteenth century," he said, "my ancestors—the Ethiopian Borana tribe known as *Gabbra*—were dying from malaria and smallpox. A plague killed their cattle and then there was no rain for two years. It was a terrible time." The chief cleared his throat.

I heard a rustling and turned to watch an ugly spotted hyena skulking into the bushes. The sly, leering way it watched us sent a twinge of uneasiness through me.

"Finally," Chief Jallaba continued, "the

British and Ethiopians forced the one remaining *Gabbra* tribe out of Ethiopia at gunpoint, and they fled to the north of Kenya, joining up with other Borana tribes. My wife and I named our daughter in honour of her grandmother. *Nagya Borana* means peace and free spirit in our language, which reminds me," he said, addressing Gabbra, "your brother completed high school in Nairobi this year with honours and, of course he makes me proud that he has become a man," beamed her father.

Nagya. I cupped my hands over my hot cheeks—I knew I was blushing. Without thinking I asked the Chief what Nagya had to do in order to become a man, and immediately regretted it, despite the fact that I had learned about circumcision from Dad.

Gabbra answered quickly, "Every year, a group of nineteen-year-old youths must travel away from the *manyatta* for a week and go through the traditional ritual of mandatory circumcision."

Our discussion was interrupted by a large herd of noisy Vulturine Guinea Fowl hopping through the bushes.

The Chief said softly, "Gabbra, you are old enough to know why I agreed to let you go to Canada with Riley." My friend leaned against the tree and looked down at her hands. I saw her glance quickly in my direction. I think she always suspected her father had kept something from her.

"From a young age you've been independent and intelligent, and you learned quickly from Nagya," he continued. "I remembered your dreams of wanting to study medicine and, although Borana girls are still not being educated, I felt you should have the chance to follow your dream."

The Chief took a deep breath. "The timing was right to get you out of the country, my daughter, and I suppose I made you an unsuspecting refugee in Canada, but I also had to get you away to escape the old tradition of female circumcision. I expected that after living in North America, you would naturally be unwilling to conform to a Borana woman's role. You would have been married two years ago if you had stayed," he said.

Shocked, I moved closer to my father. I always believed she had come to live in Canada because of *me*.

"I wanted you to know this," Gabbra's father continued, "because I made a promise to myself that after my own sister died from circumcision infection that you would never participate in this unnecessary practice."

My inquisitive nature got the better of me. "Chief, may I ask what actually happened to Gabbra's mother?" Gabbra gave a deep sigh and my father jabbed me with his elbow, which meant 'prying into personal affairs will get you into trouble'.

I thought I'd gone too far with my curiosity because Chief Jallaba stood up, glaring at me.

"Originally," he said, "Somali guerrilla bandits—called *Shifta*—raided our villages for camels, cattle and women. They sold the cattle in Kenya to buy guns and *simis,* which are very long, sharp knives. Then they buried plastic mines in sandy roads. Vehicles blew up, people were killed, and travel was extremely risky," he explained.

"We were soon engaged in a silent war with Somalia until Kenya became independent. One night these *Shifta* returned through the Dida Galgalu Plain of Darkness, and seized my wife and her sister."

The Chief looked away. Nobody moved, but at that moment, we heard a shrill, haunting sound. It was the whistling of the Acacia trees Dad told me about years ago. Black puffballs form around the thorns of Acacia trees, causing whistling noises when the wind rushes across the holes which are made by resident ants.

"I do not know whether they are still alive," the Chief murmured.

After a long moment of silence, Gabbra said quietly, "Father told me that we had suffered a severe drought, but a few days after my mother was abducted, the first drops of rain fell. In our culture it is a sign of good luck." Then she said,

"Rains always come after two years of drought, and for some mysterious reason, often after a catastrophe."

I was to remember her words in the months to come.

One of the harness systems used by tribes in
northern Kenya. (pic: Margaret Hayes)

An extremely tall termite hill.
This one could easily be 20 feet tall!

Chapter 3

COVER THAT BELLYBUTTON

LOOKING UP, I asked nobody in particular, "Are we there yet?"

"Keep your arms inside the vehicle," said the Chief, loudly. "Thorns from the Acacia trees will scratch you. Now look to your left." He pointed to a large bull giraffe, the colour of caramel and chocolate.

The evening sun threw out fingers of bronze and orange, turning termite hills into fairy-tale castles, and I noticed—with relief—the absence of a red spitting cobra, notorious for basking on warm ant hill obelisks around here. I noted in my journal that some of these architectural skyscrapers were twelve feet high and three feet wide. Perhaps the famous sculptor Michelangelo would have been impressed with these sophisticated earth masterpieces built by tiny termites.

Ignoring its audience, a tawny eagle preened itself in the middle of the road, while a lone baby camel gazed quizzically at us but carried on eating dried leaves and thorny scrub. Young boys leading camels back home for the night waved at us, but disappeared behind a cloud of dust from the LandRover.

"Be prepared for a shock, Gabbra," said Chief Jallaba. "Many of the elderly men and women have died. There is still plenty of spring water in Dumbuluk well, but our people are thin and hungry and may soon need help. Eighteen months of the worst drought I've experienced have killed off livestock and wild animals and there is no fresh pasture to be found."

He turned to my father. "Tom, the fittest and strongest of the Borana tribes in Northern Kenya and Ethiopia will survive on a diet of camel's milk and blood if necessary but, as you can see, we're getting desperate. If you agree, we'll leave tomorrow for a two-week *safari* to the north to assess the region's water situation."

Gabbra pointed out a number of fresh graves piled with stones. I suspected some of the Elders were buried there.

"We're home," she said, as we entered a stockade of thorn bushes surrounding several huts and a herd of camels.

"I won't have to drink camel's milk and blood, will I, Dad?" I asked in alarm. "Where did you put the food cooler?"

Dad grinned at me as we clambered out of the LandRover. "*You* were supposed to pack, Riley. I relied on you to do this. The cooler is probably still sitting on the doorstep in Vancouver. I have bottled water, maps, my own sleeping bag and a change of clothes. Emergency medical supplies are back in the plane. Now go and eat with Gabbra in the women's hut. I see Nagya is bringing food for the men. Goodnight Little Red Fox. I'll see you in the morning."

I overheard Chief Jallaba talking in low tones to Gabbra outside the hut. "My daughter, see that Riley is more respectfully clothed tomorrow. Her bare legs are an insult to our warriors and Elders."

Gabbra offered me a *gourd* of camel's milk but I was offended by the Chief's criticism. Tired, grimy, and fed up—partly because I had forgotten everything except my MP3 player, camera, notebook and that one melon—I grumbled that I couldn't possibly wear her clothes because they wouldn't fit me anyway.

Early next morning, Gabbra stood above me, looking down at my tousled hair. I was crabby because I'd had a sleepless night. "Gabbra, I can't sleep on the floor like this with only a camel skin for a mattress. My back is sore, and I could really use a shower and a coffee right now."

Gabbra looked refreshed. She said she'd been awake since sun-up. "Riley, I will find you a bucket of water to wash yourself. We do not serve coffee here. You'll have to settle for a piece of roast camel meat and freshly squeezed milk." I yelled at her because I was frustrated with the whole situation; she was used to my outbursts.

Dad sat on a wooden three-legged stool outside his hut, studying maps and making notes.

"Well, when are we leaving?" I asked.

He did not look up. "Riley, write your journal and take photos for your slide presentation back home. You have plenty of spare film. By the way, I hear there's a problem between you and Gabbra."

"Dad, I can't drink this stinking water. I'm definitely not eating camel meat and forget the camel milk. I need a coffee, eggs and bacon and a cosy bed to sleep in. Now let's get out of here."

My father glanced up at me from the map he was studying, narrowed his eyes and slowly removed his reading glasses. "Riley, maybe I didn't make myself clear, but I'm telling you now. In one hour, I'll be traveling north with the Chief for two weeks. Learn from Gabbra. She will take care of you, and so will Nagya. He..."

"What? Two whole weeks with that arrogant, rude warrior?" I cried, stung that Nagya hadn't come to see me since I'd arrived. "The Chief doesn't like me very much, and Gabbra is making me do disgusting chores. Remember what I promised Mom? I said I'd fight for my rights, and now she's not here to take care of me. Don't abandon me too," I sobbed, clutching his hand. "You *have* to take me with you. I won't stay here for even two days."

Dad pulled me around to face him. "Riley, I love you very much, and your mother loves you too, but you're a very stubborn and spoiled young lady and I believe you have had your own way for too long. Maybe it's time to see how people from the other side of the world live—a bit of rough hardship won't harm you."

I was startled by my father's unsympathetic decision to leave me.

"Please take me with you, Dad," I pleaded, hoping he would be more compassionate.

He held my hands together and said gently, "We're in Africa, remember? There are no fast food restaurants and no power outlets out in the bush. I believe the women are making a fire to heat water for you. There is no shower either, Riley. Soap and a face cloth are in a bag in the LandRover. You can rinse off with clean water in that bucket over there," and he pointed to a giraffe-hide container behind a tethered-up camel.

"*Fine!*" I snapped, scowling at him. He put his arm out to hug me, but I shrugged him off and stomped angrily toward the vehicle. I was conscious of Gabbra and three women peering out of the hut, staring at me, but they lowered their glare when I walked past.

Watching a cloud of dust swirling along the track, I looked up and realized that Chief Jallaba and my father had left already in the LandRover. I was miffed because Dad hadn't even said goodbye to me, and here I was, stuck in this isolated sandy hole with nothing but camel's milk and blood to survive on, nobody to talk to and a journal to write. Worst of all, Nagya was avoiding me.

Feeling miserable, I returned to my simple hut. Folding back the door flap, I stooped to get inside the windowless dome. Four people slept in the other huts, but Gabbra and I had this one to ourselves. Long sticks stuck in the ground formed a circle around a central pole; the frame was spread with semi-transparent camel hide and lashed together by leather. Early morning sunshine streamed through the walls, turning my skin a golden colour. The sand floor, freshly swept, was covered with woven grass mats, and camel-skin bedding hung outside to air. I thought about my own room back home—soft bed, comforter, huge windows, electric lights, toilet…

Now that I was truly stuck for a couple of weeks, I decided to investigate the surroundings. I crouched down to touch a freshly skinned camel hide drying in the sun—fresh material for roofing and walls of huts. It was hard like a board. On one side, blood, fat and sinew shriveled up in the heat; the reverse side had coarse hairs. The whole thing smelled revolting.

As I wandered away from the skins, I had the strange feeling I was being stalked. I looked around but all I saw were dusty thorn bushes, camels and a herd of fat-tailed sheep.

At the sound of whispering and footsteps behind me, I swirled around so fast I startled six inquisitive little boys. Aged about eight years old, they were half-naked and wearing giraffe-hair necklaces. I had never smelled such an odour before. Sweet, sweaty, pungent—not offensive but definitely part urine. They all stared at me without flinching while pulling on my hands and pawing my bare legs with their sticky little fingers.

"What are you looking at? Can't you see I'm in a bad mood?" I asked, annoyed at their shrieks of laughter.

One boy peered up at me. His twinkling eyes

were the colour of root beer and one of his ear lobes was torn into a small ragged hole. He grinned a wide toothy smile and jumped up and down in front of me, while the rest of his gang slapped their thighs with delight. When his friendly little face crinkled up with amusement, I began to relax and wished I had not been so irritated.

The jumping boy made me think back to times when I was sick or sad. I'd place my old toy Jack-in-a-box on the bed, snap open the latch and 'Jack' would leap out, grinning, springing up and down and swaying from side to side. That toy made me feel better; and so did this child. Although they couldn't understand me, I smiled and said to the one who cheered me up, "I'm not angry any more. You made me laugh, just like my Jack-in-a-box."

"*Jacky-box! Jacky-box!*" they chanted and followed me everywhere, skipping, jumping, and giggling in the shrill way that only a pack of mischievous eight-year-olds do. I left them crowding round the Jack-in-a-box boy, totally absorbed in a picture book.

Gabbra approached me with a bundle of clothes.

"I've just been attacked by a herd of kids," I said. "That one over there never keeps still—the one with the torn ear reading a book."

"That's Jillo," said Gabbra. "He's the clown

around here. He makes us laugh. He can't read but he loves looking at illustrations in the book Nagya gave him. It's the story of *Jack and the Beanstalk.*" Then she took a deep breath. "Riley, you cannot show your belly button. Shorts and tank tops are offensive to our culture. Please wear one of my *kanga* sarong tops and cover your legs with this long leather skirt."

I began to protest, "Now, just a minute, I thought I was going to wear ..."

"Also," Gabbra interrupted me, "wearing the nose stud is disrespectful in our culture. You can keep it in the leather pouch around your neck together with that clay camel of Nagya's, which I see you still wear," she said, narrowing her eyes at me. "Now come with me to the women's hut to change."

I knew better than to argue with Gabbra, and followed her silently. Ignoring my embarrassment, she told me to remove my clothes. My beautiful diamond nose stud went into the pouch. A long leather skirt was fastened firmly around my waist, but before I was fitted with a sarong, I noticed one or two older bare-breasted women.

"Gabbra," I whispered, "those women aren't wearing anything to cover their..."

"That's different. They are married," she said. "Breasts are not looked on as sexual by men. Babies need breast milk and that's it."

"Well, maybe it doesn't matter about mine then," I sulked. "Boys at school say I have mosquito bites for breasts."

Gabbra smiled broadly at me and relayed this information to the girls who chuckled like hyenas. She then knelt down on the sandy floor of the hut. Two girls held my arms and laid me gently on my back with my head resting on Gabbra's knees. She pulled my hair upward with an enormous wooden comb until it was straight, and began braiding with the help of two Borana girls.

"Ow! Ow! You're hurting! Don't yank so hard!" And the girls laughed again.

While my 'personal hairdresser' styled and braided, I looked at some of the younger girls who reminded me of Gabbra when I first met her, at thirteen years old. Their frizzy black hair was parted in the middle and fashioned into dozens of tiny thin braids hanging down to their shoulders.

"All the girls wear necklaces of patterned metal discs strung with amber, or yards of hand-made square aluminum beads," explained Gabbra. "After your hair is done, I'm going to wind these beads around your neck, six rows deep, and tie your leather pouch at the bottom of the necklace."

I asked her about the beads.

"Years ago the Mission Fathers gave my

uncle some old cooking pans. I used to watch him melt the aluminum on very high heat. Before it cooled, he'd quickly wrap the hot metal around several sticks and cut hundreds of square beads. Then he'd thread camel sinews through the hollow beads to form a five-foot long necklace," she said.

As I looked around the room, I noticed a girl resembling Gabbra standing silently at the back. She had high cheek bones, a slim nose and narrow almond-shaped black eyes, and never took her eyes off me from the moment I entered the hut. Glaring haughtily at me with arms crossed, she followed Gabbra around, but I had a very uneasy feeling about her.

"I think you can see, Riley," said Gabbra, "we are a cheerful, friendly people. My eyes were opened in Canada, but I still believe my tribal social system is the best in the world." She pulled yet another bunch of my hair with her comb.

"How can you say that, Gabbra?" I said, eyeing the unfriendly girl at the back of the hut. "Back home, we earn money for housing and food. We have a good medical system, social services and community centres. Okay, there's a high rate of divorce, drugs, crime and teen pregnancies, but our justice system is fair. We have prisons for criminals, doctors to talk to, and lawyers take care of the rest." I was in the mood for a debate.

Gabbra smiled at me. "We don't fight, or steal or become stressed. We do not tolerate sex before marriage. Women marry young and have many children, but they are faithful to their husbands. We take care of our grandparents and live together in peace. Everyone has a duty, but we rely on each other to survive."

"Well, what about religion?" I asked, determined to find a weak spot in her argument.

"My mother followed the Koran, but I guess Heaven and Earth are considered powers worthy of worship. We have a deep respect for the gifts of water and grass," said Gabbra, laughing at me because she probably thought I had nothing more to say.

I refused to surrender and continued the challenge. "If you could come back as an animal when you die, Gabbra, what would you be?" I mused, enjoying the sensuous feeling of having my head massaged.

"I don't believe in the afterlife."

"Okay, pretend then."

"A lizard or maybe a butterfly."

"Why?" I turned to look at her in surprise.

"Keep your head still, Riley," said Gabbra. "The Agama lizard around here is very colourful. It is also proud, strong, independent and secretive, and a Swallow-tail butterfly is free—everything I would like to be."

I exploded with a laugh, knowing full well

our debate had reached a truce. She tickled my cheek with the tips of her fingers like the delicate wings of a butterfly. Gabbra always made me feel happy and secure.

Two hours later, I emerged from the hut in a red sarong top, long camel-hide skirt and braids cascading down my back like a mass of writhing copper-headed snakes. I forgot my argument with Dad, and began to enjoy new friendships.

Glancing at the admiring looks of the girls, I said to Gabbra, "It was a lot of agony, but I guess it was worth it."

"We are one of the only tribes in Kenya to wear our hair long. Be proud, because now you are a true white Borana girl," she said, and interpreted this to her Borana friends.

"Gabbra, who was that tall girl in the shadows?"

"Ayasha. She…" But her explanation was lost because the girls cupped their hands over their mouths and giggled loudly at my transformation.

I was desperate to find Nagya. He had not shown up since we arrived, and I wondered why he was avoiding me. My mind was in turmoil. Now that he was a 'real man'—as Gabbra put it—maybe he didn't want to be associated with a skinny white girl with freckles on her nose and mosquito bites for breasts.

Gabbra called for me to join her with a cup of tea mixed with camel's milk. "My favourite drink! I'll be right there," I shouted back sarcastically. Instead I headed to a pile of graves outside the *manyatta*.

Dusk approached. I listened to hundreds of birds twittering and chirping before they took to their trees for the night. I felt for the pouch with my prized possessions: Nagya's clay camel and Mom's diamond nose stud. While crickets sang their never-ending serenade, I scooped up some small pebbles, aiming them at a stunted bush a few yards away. I must have frightened its residents because a family of fat sand grouse scuttled out, chuckling loudly—colourful little birds with orange and yellow throats and feathers all the way down to their toes.

I sat absolutely still, amazed at this magical land around me. I wrote whimsically in my journal that *"purple-mauve clouds lay motionless in a lilac-coloured sky; a halo of flamingo-pink surrounding a mango-yellow sun."*

Then I saw him. He stood on a rock beside a withering thorn tree, looking out toward the sinking sun—a striking silhouette of one tall, lone warrior. Nagya!

Chapter 4

PROMISES, PROMISES

WITH HIS SPEAR GLINTING, Nagya turned around and gave a fearsome yodel, beckoning me to join him on the rock. A playful smile lurked around his mouth and I stared, transfixed, into twinkling, polished-black obsidian eyes that gleamed with mischief. I noticed his bare muscular chest was thin. He wore a pair of short, cream-coloured baggy pants and a long red chequered *shuka*—man's cotton cloth—hung over one shoulder. An inner peace seemed to reflect on his chiseled features.

Astonished with the changes in his physique, I realized the sixteen-year-old boy who mocked me years ago had truly become a man.

He looked down at me for a very long time. "It is I, Nagya. I am happy to see you again, white Riley-girl. I have watched you for a long time from this rock. You are more beautiful than when we met last."

Feeling my cheeks flush with embarrassment, I tore my eyes away from his, my heart drumming double-time.

"Sit here with me, Riley-girl. I wish to hear what you and my sister have learned at private school in the last three years," said Nagya.

We sat under the Acacia tree for an hour as I recalled many social changes for Gabbra, and how well she had adjusted to the North American lifestyle. Nagya listened patiently, laughing with me, and I began to relax.

"Do you remember this leather pouch, Nagya?" I asked him. "Inside is that strange-smelling camel necklace you gave me, and my mother's diamond nose stud that Gabbra said I mustn't wear. I wore your necklace every day." I poured the contents into his palm.

"Why did you wear my necklace if it was so offensive to you?"

"Because Gabbra said it would bring bad

luck if I took it off," I lied. Nagya looked up sharply, narrowing his eyes like his sister and my father did, which meant either they didn't believe me, or they thought I was nursing a secret.

I told him how the girls stopped me in the corridor at school and whispered about Gabbra's habits. "They'd ask me if it was true the strange African girl slept on the floor by the window and drank milk and water and ate liver and kidneys. She took my dog out for long walks every evening, but nobody ever knew where she went. She never wore short skirts or jeans like the rest of us," I said.

He let me continue, gazing steadily at me, as though he was searching my face, my soul, my mind.

"Gabbra learned very fast," I told him. "On Sundays, we'd take a bus to Stanley Park. We'd sit on the grass and she'd sing about her life in Africa. People came over to us to listen."

When I finished talking, he smoothed out one of my braids and said, "You were a very impulsive thirteen-year-old, Riley, but I enjoyed teasing you because you were sharp and quick to respond. I can't do that with any of the girls here because they are taught to be submissive rather than defiant.

"I have missed my sister terribly. She's always been so dedicated in keeping the Borana tradition, and I, on the other hand, am determined it will have to change. However, three years in Canada cannot be erased, and I fear it is inevitable the promises she made to our mother cannot be kept. She probably told you about that," he said, and I nodded.

"First," he continued, "there is no future for her as an uncircumcised Borana wife whose duties include fetching water and building huts. Secondly she told me she wants to get a degree in medicine. She'd like to join Nairobi's Flying Doctors Unlimited and tend to the sick throughout Kenya. I fear she is confused right now between her duty as a Borana woman and becoming a travelling doctor."

"Then she has to make a choice," I said.

Nagya moved closer. "She also confides in our cousin who lost her mother in the same *Shifta* raid. These two girls made promises to their mothers. It's a girl thing. Daughters go through an oath-taking ceremony before they're eight years old. It's their duty to keep the culture alive," he said.

Nagya told me he had no intention of taking over the Chief's job in his tribal community. "I have been far too westernized, but I'll return to help my people when necessary. I've been accepted at a Flying School only an hour away from your home in Vancouver. After I graduate, I'd like to fly journalists, doctors and politicians to desperate areas in Kenya. My father is proud of me, and he respects my decisions. I want to make a difference in my part of the world. One day I shall tell you my dreams and plans for the future. For now, it's up to me and my father to convince the Elders that change is inevitable. Tell me about yourself, Riley-girl," he said.

I told him of my own promise to my mother, how she had left when I was eight years old. "It's hard to try and change the world when you're a teenager but I know people sit up and listen to what I have to say."

"Yes, you certainly can talk! But tell me what you do best."

Annoyed, I continued. "Gabbra says I'm an activist. I fight for people's rights and…"

"Like what?"

"Well, I'm head of the Student Council and fight for students' concerns like more bottled water machines and less junk food. I campaign against racists, bullies, and marijuana-smoking, so I'm also trying to make a difference in a small way. Gabbra says the teachers think I'm a powerful speaker, but opinionated, and all the kids in class nicknamed me 'Red Robin Hood Riley' because I get people to empty their wallets for worthy fundraising campaigns."

Nagya rested his hand on my bare shoulder and threw back his head with amusement. The creases around his eyes were like black slits as he laughed. "Perhaps it's not just North America you'll change, Riley-girl, but a place like this. I see a drastic shift in tradition coming, and you've definitely made an impression on our young people."

I glanced down and caught a look at Nagya's weird-looking shoes.

"I can run faster in these sandals than my sneakers," he said, noticing my curiosity. Nagya told me he had found an old blown-out tire on the side of the road in Nairobi. Together, he and a school mate dragged the tire back to school and, using a sharp knife, shaped two pairs of soles from the thick rubber tire. Then, for each shoe, they cut out two thin strips from inner tubing to criss-cross over the front and a wide band to hold the heel in place. The straps were stapled to the sole.

"I can walk miles in these extreme all-weather rubber sandals," he said, grinning at me. "If you like, I'll make you a pair."

Nagya stood up suddenly and pointed his spear into the distance. "Look, here comes the last household camel."

Kicking up clouds of dust, the lone camel looked like a creature from *Star Wars* as it trudged in the sandy plain. A curved stick frame balanced high above its hump, ready to hold a lot of cargo. Nagya said his extended family uprooted everything they owned to look for fresh pasture—difficult to find during a drought. Secondly, tradition dictates that during circumcision practices, the *manyatta* again must be moved.

He brought out the impulsiveness in me. "And what would happen if you decided not to be...you know...circumcised?" I asked.

"I have just returned from the ceremony which, by the way, isn't dangerous like it is for girls. If I had declined the circumcision ritual, I would have hurt my father's feelings. I have reached one of the most important age-grades of a Borana male and proven myself worthy of his respect," explained Nagya. He looked at me so intently that I dared not interrupt him.

"We traveled far away from the *manyatta* for the circumcision ritual. Afterwards, we slaughtered camels and ate camel meat for four days and slept under a tree. When the sun rose on the fifth day, the girls were allowed to join us and we danced and sang together until the new moon was sighted," continued Nagya.

"But why haven't you come inside to sleep?" I asked, fascinated.

"I will tonight," he replied. "The Elder women invite us back to the *manyatta*. All the fresh camel skins have been spread out to dry and any meat that we warriors could not eat is given to our families. The women are preparing for a celebration dance tonight to welcome us home."

"More dancing?"

"Yes," he said. "The Chief and Elders talked

to us last night about marital rules and have given each of us permission to choose a wife at this ceremony. You should see how we men preen ourselves. Shall I give you details about the actual circumcision operation?"

I felt myself panicking. "No! Stop right there, Nagya."

He grinned at my discomfort. "I hope I will see you later at the dance, Riley-girl. Tell Gabbra to bring you."

The tiny cowrie shells on the bottom of my leather skirt swished and clicked gently as I skipped happily back to the *manyatta* alone.

Later that night, Gabbra and I sauntered over to the traditional ceremonial feast and dance. I sat with her, watching several provocative teenage girls from the *manyatta* hoping to catch the eye of a prospective husband. They didn't look submissive to me, I thought, remembering Nagya's explanation of how young Borana women were supposed to behave.

As soon as Nagya took the ceremonial cup of beer with his father and other decorated menfolk, drumming became louder and more frantic, dancing more uninhibited and frenzied. Women singers ululated—a special high warbling sound made by rapidly flexing their tongues up and down with their mouths wide open.

As Nagya shuffled wildly in front of the girls, a shower of dust particles cascaded like fine jewels in the firelight. His body glistened with sweat and his face was alive with excitement as he threw his arms out in delirium.

The dancers swayed with half-closed eyes, hypnotized by the rhythm of the drums. Warriors circled around the girls, jumping and leaping with knees bent, touching the girls' breasts before being pushed gently away.

Then Nagya laid his hands on the shoulders of one girl and looked deep into her eyes. It was Ayasha, the same silent, unsmiling, arrogant girl I saw in the women's hut when Gabbra braided my hair. Ayasha was beautiful. Her skin shone over high cheek bones, just like Gabbra's. She wore a wispy white cloth over her head and shoulders. Yards of silver aluminum beads hung down her chest, nestling into the already-firm cleavage of her breasts. And for the first time I saw her smile.

"You witch!" I said out loud, feeling jealous and humiliated.

Tormented, I watched flames darting like venomous tongues, as sparks flew from the crackling fire.

Gabbra nudged me gently. "Don't move, Riley." A foot away from where I was sitting, a long sand snake slithered to the safety of a bush and curled up on a bare branch. I shivered with fright and was reminded of the Greek mythology

I'd studied at school. *Medusa* was the beautiful woman with snakes for hair, but was so mean and cold that anyone who looked at her was turned to stone.

"I'll call you *Medusa*," I muttered, angrily.

"Who are you calling *Medusa*?" asked Gabbra loudly over the din of banging drums.

"That snake over there." Reasoning with myself, I tried to understand why I felt so upset. Nagya was from another world—a community tribesman with western upbringing. I was a Canadian girl in Africa, with a crush on the son of a Borana chief.

Annoyed, I left Gabbra dancing with a tall warrior, and stomped back to my hut without bothering to tell anyone. I lay awake all night, my stomach churning with thoughts of Nagya and Ayasha. He ignored me at the dance and it hurt after our warm and friendly discussion on the rock. I wrapped the scratchy camel skin around my shoulders and must have dozed off.

I woke up when I heard the hollow sound of wooden bells clapping. The camels were kicking up sand noisily with their floppy feet and settled down, with soft, jingly thuds, to rest.

Gabbra crept into the hut and lay beside me, jabbering wearily. "He loves to dance. It's two hours to sun-up and we must fetch water today. We missed you, Riley." And she fell asleep.

Chapter 5

GABBRA'S SONG

WE DID NOT REST FOR LONG. At crack of
dawn, the sun crept over the plains and woke up
both birds and Boranas.

I poked my head out of the hut. Nagya was
untying several camels. "Good morning, Riley-girl.
I looked for you last night, but you disappeared. I
think you dumped me."

When I opened my mouth to say something,
he called out, "It's been five days since the family

went for water, so we're getting ready for a long trek to the Singing Well of Dumbuluk. Bring a water container and tell Gabbra to cut off a chunk of camel's meat for a snack."

Jillo, my little jumping friend with the torn ear, appeared, just as Nagya hoisted Gabbra and myself on top of a camel. Jillo tapped our camel on the front feet with a stick and I tried to keep my balance as the beast came up first with its back legs and then the front.

Jillo took the lead, pulling the camel by a rope threaded through a pierced hole in its nostrils. Strong men, women and teenage girls walked beside their camels behind Jillo, each animal bulging with large empty clay pots strapped on both sides with leather ties. Nagya took up the rear with a menacing-looking camel.

"*Clack! Clack! Clackity-Clack!*" I made up a song in time to the clapping and clunking of the wooden camel bells hanging around their necks. Camels have a strange walk, they move both their left feet forward and then both right in a rolling motion as they walk. They only have two toes on each foot.

"These animals are hilarious," I said to Gabbra, "I feel like I'm being tossed around on a ship in a storm." I looked over my shoulder at Nagya, who never took his eyes off me.

We trekked in the hot sun for a slow two hours through a sea of rocks, grassy plains and thorny Acacia trees, while Gabbra pointed out a herd of giraffes and gazelles camouflaged in the thickets of prickly thorn bushes. Ahead of us, camels kicked up clouds of dust with their big feet, and we swatted those darn flies.

"Cover your eyes," shouted Nagya. There's a dust devil coming." A sudden gust of wind moaned right over us, lifting a column of sand that danced and twisted like an angry snake before disappearing into the distance. I felt like I'd been slapped hard on the cheeks, my eyes stung and we were covered in a fine coating of sand.

"It wasn't a big one," said Nagya, "Sometimes we have to get down behind the camels to protect ourselves. Camels can handle these storms; if you look closely, they have a third eyelid they can see through, and they can also close their nostrils."

"Then why do they have such ridiculously tiny ears and such a huge, long head?" I asked.

"Their ridiculous ears, as you put it, serve a useful purpose. They have little hairs inside them which help keep dust and sand out, Riley." By the stern look on his face, I knew better than to ask more opinionated questions.

A well-worn track of animal dung led us down a steep hill and into a dusty valley. I noticed several families waiting for water. Each group of camels, mules, cattle and fat-tailed sheep munched on spiky dried leaves while waiting outside a circle of thorny bushes.

"Get off your camel, girls, and sit under that thorn tree where it's cool," said Nagya. "We have to wait a long time for our turn to draw water."

When I asked why the livestock had to stay on the other side of the thorn bushes, Nagya told me that otherwise the animals would foul up both the well area and the water trough.

Reaching for my bag, I took out the warm melon I had been saving. Pulling it open with my fingers, I shared the messy, over-ripe fruit with Gabbra, Nagya and Jillo, savouring every drop of sweet juice that dripped from the flesh. Jillo ate the skin and carefully picked out the slimy tan-coloured seeds I had discarded in the sand. He shoved the whole lot quickly into his shirt pocket and scurried over to join the young herds boys perched on a tree trunk growing sideways out of a rock. They sat on their haunches, chests resting on their knees, spears propped up against the tree. A bundle of grubby cloth *shukas* hung over a branch, apparently to keep the boys warm on cold evenings. Delighted to break the boredom of perching and waiting, the youngsters jumped down from the tree trunk, swarming over Jillo's seedy treasure.

Squinting in the sun, I followed Gabbra and the girls, and sat in the shade of a large Acacia tree, while one family after another took turns entering the thorn enclosure and drawing spring

water from Dumbuluk's natural underground well.
I felt dirty and sweaty and could not get the smell
of camel dung out of my nose. The stink of rancid
camel grease around my aluminum beaded
necklace was making me nauseous too.

"Riley, I will teach you how to play an
ancient African game called *mbau*," said Gabbra.
She dug into her skin bag and brought out a piece
of wood with two rows of eight small 'dishes'
hollowed out side-by-side along its length.

"We both start with a certain quantity of
small pebbles or hard seeds, which we'll call our
herd of camels. It's a pick-up-and-leave game, and
the idea is to go around the board, poaching all
the other person's camels and herding them over
to your own place. I liked this game when I was
younger because it taught me how to count and I
got quite good at it."

"Does Nagya play this game?" I asked her.

"Yes. And he is very good, but he'd rather
play a kind of desert roulette using scorpions."

"What if he got stung?"

"You have to be very quick! First you draw a
circle in the sand, then you identify your scorpion
and put the other contestants in the middle,
pushing them around to make them dizzy. They
stagger about and if your scorpion stays in the
circle without leaving, you win."

By the time I'd learned how to play *mbau*, we
had an audience of several teenage girls screaming

excitedly when Gabbra poached all my camels. Feeling miffed at losing all the time, I told Gabbra I was bored and began drawing squares in the sand.

"I have a game," I announced to everyone. "It's called hopscotch. See, you toss a pebble into one of the squares, then hop on one foot, grab the pebble and hop back to the beginning. It gets harder as you go along."

My leather clothes were hindering me from showing the girls how to play the game, but as I hitched the cumbersome skirt to my thighs they giggled at either my bare legs or the ungainly way I was hopping from square to square.

"Gabbra, it's very difficult to jump in this skirt," I moaned.

"If you stop complaining, I'll translate the game to these girls."

I had shown Gabbra how to play hopscotch at home when she was thirteen years old. She made up new ways to play using coloured chalk to fill in all the squares, and my Canadian friends, fascinated by this new bronze-skinned kid, chanted rhythms when it was her turn to hop:

"Gabbra, Gabbra,
Abbra-Cadabra!
If she lands on Red —
She'll fall down dead!"

Nagya came over to see what all the laughter was about. "It will soon be our turn to take the camels down for water. They are impatient because they can see the water trough through the thorn hedge," he said over the deafening sound of agitated camels bellowing and moaning.

"I'm impressed with the sheriff guy at the entrance of the hedge," I said to Nagya. I pointed to an old man wearing a dirty turban wound high around his head and a *shuka* slung across his shoulders. His arms hung over each end of a long stick balanced horizontally behind his neck. He wore dozens of aluminum bangles up each arm and plugs of bone in his stretched earlobes. His fine-featured face was lined and furrowed from squinting at the sun, and as he yelled out orders at restless animals and thirsty herders, his white fluffy beard and moustache waggled from side to side.

Nagya chuckled, presumably at my interpretation of Borana regimentation. "Animals have to be controlled or there would be a stampede and people killed. The old man taps the camels on the nose with a stick when they start getting too restless."

"Nagya, why are those young kids allowed to handle spears?" I asked, looking at Jillo and his friends.

"Not only are herding boys responsible for looking after our camels, they use spears to threaten attacking wild animals and..."

A sudden high whistling sound came from behind the hedge.

"Okay! Let's go! It's our turn!" shouted Nagya. "The old man is beckoning us."

The camels charged, stampeding in anticipation down the narrow path to the well, fine white dust and swarms of black flies swirling up behind them, blinding the herds boys trying to control their animals. Out through a pathway in another direction, the previous herd of thin cattle, donkeys and camels thundered up from the well, water dripping and frothing from their mouths. I recalled Nagya saying camels could drink thirty gallons of water in ten minutes.

From the shade of a thorn tree, I took photographs of Nagya organizing the herd, boys running with wooden cups to capture the precious water, and young Borana girls, with glowing skins and braided hair, struggling with huge water containers strapped to their backs.

I walked through the thorn entrance to get a better view of three camels jostling for water from the trough. Their long necks pointed downward together, soft hairy muzzles twitching, while wooden bells around their necks made hollow thudding sounds as they slurped and snorted noisily. They were so close together that one camel's eye was pressing against the other's eye socket. I laughed out loud at the thought of my photo showing a three-headed camel.

Gabbra stood on the lip of the well and waved at me, then she disappeared from sight. My heart lurched.

"Gabbra! Gabbra, what are you doing?" I shrieked. Had she fallen down the well?

Running down to her, I forced my way between the camels' long necks as they sloshed and splashed messily from the trough, dripping water and saliva from their rubber-like mouths.

Disturbing a flock of doves, I leaned over the well and looked down a hole about thirty feet deep. Young men and women hung onto each other from a home-made wooden ladder roped together with strips of leather and wedged between rocks that jutted out all the way down.

Gabbra had gone.

I strained my eyes to see if there was a body at the bottom, but nobody was in the least bit concerned. Then came the sweetest sound I had ever heard. I forgot the stink of animal dung.

"It's Gabbra!" I murmured. Her pure, unfaltering voice warbled and trilled like a nightingale, echoing from the bottom of the well. I closed my eyes wondering why there was a strange lump in my throat, then my eyes welled up and hot tears splashed down my cheeks. Gabbra's sweet singing had brought back swift, emotional memories of my mother singing me to sleep when I was little.

Fascinated, I watched as giraffe-hide buckets—three at a time—were filled and passed from hand to hand up the well in a rhythmic movement, and poured into the trough above. Empty ones were sent down, reminding me of a juggling act at the circus. Bare-chested young men hummed like the buzzing of bees, while older men sang in low tones. Further down the well I heard women chanting eerily in high-pitched voices. It was a *singing* well with a full concert of bass, treble and soprano voices.

Up came the men and young girls, followed by older bare-breasted women wearing layers of aluminum and amber necklaces, and brass bangles all the way up their arms. Finally, Gabbra emerged, looking deliriously happy.

"Riley, you've been crying. Wait, I'm coming over to hug you," she said, clambering across the edge of the well and jumping across the trough to the ground.

"You're soaking wet, Gabbra," I laughed through my tears. "I thought you had fallen down the well and drowned."

"I climbed down and scooped up the first *gourd* of water and passed it up to the next person," she said. "I sang praises exactly how my mother taught me. I'm very happy because I know in my heart she has forgiven me for breaking the promises I made to her."

A shadow fell over us. Ayasha crossed her

arms and looked coldly at us both. She said nothing and walked away.

"I don't like that girl." I scowled at Gabbra. "There's something wicked..."

"Oh, don't worry about her, she's a little bit crazy, but she means well and she's very important to us," said Gabbra. "You're probably wondering why we are not filling up our *kibuyus,* our water containers. We let the livestock drink first, then we get the herds boys to take care of the animals and wait for us while the women fill the containers."

I watched as Nagya helped load the *kibuyus* into baskets attached to the sides of camels. Gabbra said baskets were made of palm fronds, dried mud and dung and on long journeys, mothers would even place their sleeping babies inside empty baskets.

In order to get himself heard above the bellowing of the camels, Nagya began shouting orders to the herds boys. Then he turned to me and said with anxiety in his voice, "We have to leave right away. Never risk camels getting chills at night. They'll be unable to work. Besides, lions and hyenas lurk around here sometimes and the camels will panic and run away if they sense danger. We must keep moving until we reach the *manyatta.*"

Jillo helped me get onto the camel's back. I took a liking to this friendly little boy because he seemed to want to take care of me.

I studied the way Nagya threaded ropes of leather and strong dry grass underneath the belly of my camel. He reached over its hump, tying the water pots securely on either side and around the base of the camel's tail to keep everything stabilized.

"Must be uncomfortable for the camel," I muttered as Jillo went ahead of us.

"What? The grass thong under his tail?" Nagya grinned at me, tapping his camel to get up.

"Never mind!" I scowled at him.

"Well, while we're on the subject, I should educate you on the sexual habits of the camel," Nagya said. "It's an incredible sight to see."

"I don't wish to know, thank you."

"When the female is in heat," Nagya continued, ignoring my protest, "the male smells her. He growls and drools. His tongue turns black and blue, double its normal size, like a balloon or a bladder hanging out the side of his mouth."

"Nagya! That's disgusting!"

"He blows bubbles of saliva and snot when he gets excited," said Nagya, adding spice to my revulsion. "But if he's annoyed, he gets extremely aggressive, biting with his huge teeth and swinging his neck like a sledge hammer..."

"Nagya, I've heard enough!"

There was no stopping him. "He'll reach round and bite you if you're on his back, and throw you off, then he'll rear up on his hind legs, knock you down and spit regurgitated food in your face."

"I'll try not to irritate a camel then," I said and turned around quickly so he wouldn't see my embarrassment. But even Gabbra's shoulders shook from laughing.

The undulating movement on top of the camel made me drowsy but I didn't want to fall asleep. It was a long way down if I fell, and I definitely did not relish the thought of my camel slobbering over me.

Back at the *manyatta*, Nagya sang as he pulled water pots off the camels, and called for the young girls. Without a word, females—both young and old—steadied jugs on their heads with their hands and walked carefully to each hut.

"In Canada, women have rights. Why don't those lazy herding kids help?" I asked Nagya, pointing at Jillo and a group of boys playing tag in the sand.

"It's not their work," said Nagya, curtly. "You have to understand that herding camels, tending to livestock and drawing blood from camels for refreshment is boys' work. Girls' work is looking after children, milking camels, cooking meat, carrying water jugs, and building huts."

I glared at him. "I thought you knew about

our western ways. Usually men and women share
household chores if they both work. Sometimes
men will take care of the children and do the
housework while women bring home the pay
cheque. And you've seen women doing men's
work like gas attendants, astronauts, engineers,
pilots..."

Nagya interrupted me. "We get along as a
team here but we all have our jobs to do," he said
firmly. "Riley, my sister is calling for you from the
women's hut. This is the only life they know. I
can see you're in for one of your famous debates,
so we'll have to continue our discussion on culture
shock tomorrow." And he trudged over to the
men's hut.

Later that night, Gabbra and I sat close
together and drank tea made with camel's milk. I
was beginning to like this soothing drink.

"Gabbra, why do you get to sing down the
well, and nobody else?" I asked.

She turned her head quickly to look at me.
"Young Borana children are educated through
music and singing, and taught to value traditions.
Only one girl who has a special quality of voice
and is still a virgin can purify the water. They say
my voice is like a lullaby because it calms fidgety
children and soothes angry camels. Our chanting
is like a hymn—we are always asking Heaven and
Earth for rain, grass, milk and peace. It's magical
at the bottom of the well, and I feel honoured to

have been chosen. But today, I added personal praises to my mother," she said, quietly.

"Will you teach me how to sing your beautiful song, Gabbra?"

"Yes, my talkative friend. I promise to teach you Gabbra's Song."

I decided I would climb down one day and see for myself what she found so wonderful at the bottom of the Dumbuluk Singing Well.

Teenage girls carrying baskets containing
gourds of water on their backs.

Married woman near the bottom of Dumbuluk well.

Chapter 6

BANDITS IN THE NIGHT

THE MOON WAS HIGH THAT NIGHT as I
sat at the entrance of our hut. It was difficult to
sleep with the deafening trill of a million crickets
and the distant barking of baboons.

I could see the camels lying with their legs
folded beneath them, huffing small rings of steam
into the cold air. I shivered, even though I'd
draped Nagya's *shuka* over my head and shoulders
to keep warm.

"Riley, what's the matter? Can't you sleep?" said Gabbra in a sleepy voice from the bed. "Don't stay out too long."

"Nagya's sitting on his special lookout hill," I replied softly. "Does he stay there all night?"

"Well, someone has to. It's his turn to keep guard. He can see all around from that hill."

I watched Nagya wrap a camel skin blanket tightly around himself, and I yearned to sit beside him.

How did he feel about me? About Ayasha? I wondered.

I crept into bed and tried to relax, finally drifting into a deep sleep. I dreamed I was on a boat with Gabbra and Nagya. As the waves became bigger and stronger, a massive serpent snatched Gabbra and dragged her under the sea. My legs were heavy like cement as I tried to jump overboard to save her, but when the boat turned upside down I knew we were all going to drown and I woke up screaming.

Gabbra shook me roughly by the shoulders. "Stop hitting me, Riley. You're having a nightmare. Get up now. We must run to the safety tunnel. The *Shifta* are here."

I sat up quickly and grabbed her hand. "What do you mean, Gabbra? I dreamed you were drowning. *Shifta*? How do you know they're here?"

"Listen," she said, cupping one hand to her ear. From Nagya's hill came the loud, repetitive song of a mourning dove.

"It's Nagya, warning us the bandits are approaching the *manyatta*. Now let's go," she urged.

Following Gabbra quietly out of the hut, I saw spears glinting in the moonlight as one by one the Borana warriors, together with several older tribesmen, jogged swiftly to join Nagya on the hill.

Always seeming to be in control, Gabbra led sleepy children, mothers with babies on their backs and the elderly men and women quietly to a big pile of dry thorn bushes. She wound a large cloth around her hand and, pulling the thorns to one side, took her people down a narrow tunnel into a twelve-foot-square area.

Feeling frightened and uneasy in this depressing pit, I stumbled blindly, moving my hands along the side of a damp, dirt wall until I found an empty spot and sat down. It was humid and claustrophobic down there, with an odour of musty old potatoes. The smell of rancid milk and pungent body sweat was disgusting.

In the darkness, I heard mothers crooning softly to their whimpering children and the unmistakable sound of babies suckling. I remembered watching a woman nurse her baby in public back home. The woman had pulled a shawl over herself and the child, but I still felt offended by that embarrassing slurping noise. Yet here in Africa, it seemed perfectly natural for mothers to offer naked breasts to their demanding infants.

Now in the pitch-black tunnel, I felt a pair of small hands groping my hair and face. A naked child squirmed on my lap, spreading his legs on either side of my thighs. Pushing his sticky fingers under my *kanga* top, he probed around until he found my nipples. I stiffened; utterly horrified. He smelled so strongly of urine and camel dung that I wrinkled my nose in disgust, hardly able to breathe.

Panic brought back a memory of me as a four-year-old playing hide-and-seek when my younger cousin and I had hidden inside a dark cupboard and couldn't get out. Terrified, we screamed and kicked the door until somebody heard us, but I never forgot the smell of urine and vomit we left inside that cupboard.

Down in the tunnel, I called desperately for Gabbra. "I'm getting out of here. I need air," I said in a small voice.

"Stay where you are," whispered Gabbra. "If the bandits find us down here, it could be nasty. Just be patient and think positive thoughts."

The reassuring grip of her hand on my wrist instilled a fresh confidence in me. "I'm going to pull the bushes over the top of the entrance," she said.

I felt a hot surge of dampness spread along my thighs. The toddler had just peed on me. He wriggled to a drier spot on my lap and flung his little arms tightly around my neck, snuggling his warm, wet body closer to me. As he planted his soft lips on my cheek, I stroked his head hesitatingly, and pulled him closer to my chest. I was surprised at the sudden rush of emotion I felt. If this was the maternal instinct we giggled and scoffed at in Sex Ed at school, then I think I started understanding what the instructor had been talking about.

Gabbra broke my thoughts. Although I could not see, I heard her singing soothingly to each mother and child. Her hand brushed my arm and the child on my lap.

"I didn't know you had such motherly feelings," said Gabbra. "The baby's mama says she is grateful to you for taking care of her son. Anyway, I've brought you another friend. He's been looking for you."

It was Jillo, my Jack-in-a-box boy. He felt for my free hand and never left my side in that dank dungeon.

I sensed Gabbra still crouching in front of me. Her breath was warm and sweet as she sang softly to comfort us, and I realized I was not afraid when Gabbra was near.

"Gabbra," I whispered, "Are we going to die

down here?"

"Riley, why must you talk all the time? Questions, always questions. You can't stand silence, can you!" she answered in hushed tones, but she chuckled. "We're not going to die, my friend. Nagya is very brave. He and his warriors will fight to the death to save us."

What if I left this world and Nagya never knew how I felt about him? "Gabbra, I have a secret," I blurted out, wildly. "I'd really miss Nagya. I want you to tell him that, if something happens to me. Do you have secrets, Gabbra?"

"I'd miss learning more about western medicine."

"I mean a *real* secret," I insisted, arching my back to try and shake off the baby's mouth that was again trying to find my breast.

"Well, there's this guy called Sam..." she said, stopping mid sentence. Gabbra drew in her breath sharply.

"Who is Sam?" I hissed.

"Okay, you caught me off-guard. I've fallen in love with a Somali medical student in Vancouver. We're both planning on returning to Kenya as members of the Flying Doctors Unlimited," she said.

I was speechless.

"Riley, *you're* not saying anything."

"I'm shocked, that's all."

"He wears my grandfather's gold ring—the

one with the lion's head engraved on it," said Gabbra. "Now I've told you too much."

"You'll never be allowed to marry a Somali," I said.

"I'll just go and see what's happening," she said, evasively, and disappeared up the tunnel.

Gabbra returned a few minutes later. "It's horrible," she whispered in a shaky voice. "At first I heard gun shots and clash of *simis*. There was so much angry yelling, the camels were bawling. Now there is silence. I fear for our warriors. We must be ready to tend to the wounded."

Although I could not see her face, I knew she was anxious and that's what made me nervous.

"What happened? Is there blood?" I asked, beginning to panic.

"I called to an injured warrior lying just outside the tunnel. He stayed to protect us. He told me everything while I hid under the canopy," Gabbra said.

She explained that the warrior saw many bandits sneaking through the *manyatta* entrance but they were surprised by Borana warriors already waiting for them. The *Shifta* were attacked and held back but some of them poked their rifles through the thorn enclosure and shot three or four of the Boranas.

"The warrior I spoke to said he had been hit by a stray bullet but he crawled over to the tunnel to make sure we were safe," said Gabbra. "Keeping a tight grip on his *simi*, he lay in the sand as he watched from a distance. A fierce-looking bandit had torn off his shirt to wrap tightly around his bleeding leg," she explained.

Gabbra said the warrior saw the wounded bandit searching all the women's huts. When he came out empty-handed, he yelled angrily to his band members and limped out of sight. A few minutes later he rode out of the *manyatta* on a camel, followed by several injured Somalis escaping with stolen Borana livestock and supplies.

"Our men are badly hurt—many seriously—and they'll need our help," said Gabbra. "You have to be brave, Riley. Some of the *Shifta* have been killed but the rest are probably hiding out in the Plain of Darkness with many of our camels, freshly-cured camel skins and water containers. It's over two hundred miles to the Somali border, and I'll bet these bandits will collapse before they get there. Our warriors were too strong for them. Come, let's go. I think it's safe now."

The baby clung onto my neck, his legs wrapped tightly around my waist while Jillo kept very close behind me. Using one hand to feel my way along, I hitched up my skirt, crawling blindly along the tunnel. A blast of light hit me in the

face, making my eyes squint. Unaccustomed to
the early morning brightness, I bumped my head
against the bare feet of a young girl in front of
me. Turning her head slowly, Ayasha glared icily
at me and I clutched the little boy instinctively to
my chest.

She was like a dull headache that wouldn't go
away.

A young woman carrying a newborn infant
approached me at the top of the tunnel.
Reluctantly I handed the little boy over to his
mother. She smiled and laid a hand on my head,
which I took as a gesture of thanks.

And Jillo? He stood by my side until he
heard several urgent whistles from his friends, and
ran off to tend camels. I stood beside Gabbra,
feeling useless and frightened.

Young girls ran to the nearest hut and
returned with bowls of boiled water while Gabbra
and the women tended to the warriors. I stood
over her as she knelt beside one young man who
was bleeding badly.

"They're so brave, Gabbra. They're hurt but
not even one of them is screaming in agony," I
said, feeling squeamish.

My friend looked up at me. "Warriors do not
groan in pain because they are now men and any
form of weakness shows cowardice."

I watched her and the women as they carried *gourds* of boiled water to the injured men, using fresh *shukas* to clean the wounds. Gabbra soothed the men with her singing. She was organized, efficient, and totally in control.

One warrior gave a gasp and then died. I stared, horrified to see death for the first time. His eyes seemed to turn inside-out. Scarlet-and-black blood oozed and gurgled from his mouth and then he stopped breathing and lay still. One of the women threw her hands into the air and swayed from side to side, moaning in anguish.

The smell of sweat and blood, the sight of torn flesh and the agonized wail of the women were more than I could bear. That queasy sensation swamped me again.

"Nagya! Where are you? Are you still alive?" I screamed hysterically. My mouth filled with acidic saliva and my head pounded. Staggering weakly to a scraggly bush, I fell on my hands and knees and retched until nothing was left inside my stomach. Sobbing uncontrollably I called out, "Gabbra, help me. I don't feel very well."

Gabbra beckoned one of the women to take over for her and, pulling me toward her, hugged me tightly, wiping the vomit from my mouth with a clean *shuka.*

"Riley, listen to me. You must be brave. You are disturbing my sick patients with your wailing. If you cannot help, then please go away and find a quiet place to sit. Otherwise, bring a large *gourd* of boiling water from the fire and set it beside me. Drink this tea first. It will calm you down." She told me it was her own mixture of dried flowers picked from our garden in Vancouver, to treat panic and shock. She handed me a wooden bowl filled with a sweet-smelling broth and I held it to my quivering lips.

"I thought you said we wouldn't die," I shouted at her. "Your father said *Borana* means peace, but I don't find this a very peaceful way of living at all."

"You have to understand something," Gabbra continued. "Although we live in danger and much hardship, we take care of one another, just as you did with that baby on your lap, with Jillo at your side trying to protect you. I told you before, that's why we've survived all these years." Pointing to a nearby tree, she added, "Nagya is still alive, but badly wounded. I've got to go to him."

Drinking the tea was a brief reminder of a similar experience I'd had when I was nine years old, after being bitten on the ankle by a small grey scorpion on a cattle ranch in Kenya where my father had taken me to visit friend. It felt like a fork had been jammed into my foot, and I screamed in agony as sharp needles of poison shot up into my groin. I began to shake uncontrollably and my teeth wouldn't keep still as

I asked the wrinkled old rancher if I was going to die. His reply was: "Just drink this and I promise you won't feel any pain." He handed me a cup of warm herbal tea sweetened with honey, and I remembered that same relaxed feeling as the sharp tingling of pins-and-needles in my leg gradually subsided.

Feeling ashamed of myself for the outburst, but soothed and energized from the tea, I walked back to the hut and returned with a *gourd* of boiling water.

Gabbra took out a few strange-looking dried leaves from a leather bag. "These are special healing leaves—wild *banghi* or *cannibus.*"

I stared at her, knowing full well what that was. I opened my mouth to object to a practice I was passionately against, but she explained quickly, "Riley, it's been handed down from tribe to tribe for thousands of years and used as a mild anesthetic during emergencies like this. Now go down to the hut and throw the leaves into the fire. Inhale the smoke deeply for a few minutes. You'll feel better—it'll give you a slight euphoric feeling."

I did as she instructed and after a few minutes of sniffing the heavy musk-sweet fragrance, I began to relax. Nagya lay motionless but still breathing. He was bleeding profusely from gashes to his chest and legs, and winced while Gabbra pushed a long thorn from the

Acacia tree through both edges of torn flesh. A fine fibrous thread—stripped from tree bark—was wound around both ends of the thorn to hold the wound together.

Now I wasn't scared or nauseous any more. I kept myself busy carrying water over to the women.

Then Gabbra smeared a thick layer of honey over Nagya's injury. "Why are you putting honey on him?" I asked.

"Honey acts as a natural antibiotic," she explained. Gabbra probably noticed a look of skepticism on my face. "Dung from the fire is used to smoke out the bees, then we gather the honey and wax from the hive and store it in a large container. After the wound is stitched up and covered with honey, it is protected by absorbent boiled bark from the Acacia tree, just like a soft leather bandage," she said.

Kneeling beside Nagya I brushed my lips impulsively against his cheek and stroked his sweating forehead.

A shadow fell over Nagya's face and Ayasha appeared with her arms crossed, staring down at us.

Nagya's eyes flickered open and he gazed up at me. He tried to talk so I put my ear near his mouth. "Stay with me, Riley-girl," he said, squeezing my hand and smiling weakly.

When Gabbra beckoned some time later, it

was with reluctance that I left Nagya.

"Riley," Gabbra whispered, sounding exhausted, "I'm in despair because I don't know what to do. I can't let my people know that I'm anxious, but I'm worried that unless I get proper medicine to our warriors, they'll die of infection and tetanus. Their wounds are deep from the bandits' sharp *simis* and I realize the natural healing power of honey and protective tree bark is not enough. If only I could contact the Flying Doctors in Nairobi. Both our fathers are traveling in the LandRover where the radio-call set is kept."

I sucked in my breath. My brave and proud friend had never shown fear before. She was the one to comfort and sing soothingly in times of distress; it was she who took control when my temper tantrums got out of hand. The only time she showed her emotion was on the plane, and that was a feeling of pride that her brother had reached an important stage in life.

"I have to talk to you Riley, because I can't tell anyone else. I wish my father was here," she sighed, pushing strands of hair from her face.

Beside us a young warrior tried to grasp Gabbra's hand. He shuddered weakly and then fell still, eyes wide open. I will never forget the buzzing sound of big black flies swarming greedily into the dead man's open wounds.

Gabbra walked over to Nagya, laid her head on his chest and wept.

A young Borana boy very much like Jillo.

Young boys herding camels.
(pics: Margaret Hayes)

Chapter 7

WILD RIDERS

NAGYA WAS TERRIBLY WEAK. One more warrior had to be buried and the rest lay motionless and barely conscious. Although Gabbra looked exhausted, she would not rest. She washed their wounds and stitched up deep gashes with the Acacia thorns, singing her soothing songs and instructing the women to search for more tree bark.

Lost in thought, I continued the

monotonous job of filling up my *gourd* with hot water and trudging back to the injured men.

Our camels refused to lie down after the attack. They pounded the ground nervously with their big soft feet while the hot mid-morning sun turned a peach colour from the haze of grey dust that the camels had kicked up. Gabbra sang to the animals to quiet them and stroked their velvety muzzles until they relaxed and folded up their legs on the ground ready for sleep.

Our water supply was becoming dangerously low, but as a precaution against possible lurking bandits, the herds boys were told not to take the camels out of the *manyatta* until the following day, when they could ride to the well and fill the remaining empty containers that the *Shifta* did not take.

Jillo played in the sand with his friends. He and another boy looked up at me and wandered over to the fire. They pulled me by both hands and began to lead me toward the entrance of the *manyatta*.

Grateful for a break from the exhausting job of carrying water, I told the boys to wait while I ran to get my camera from the hut and followed them to a ten-foot-high termite tower outside the thorn hedge of the enclosure.

With sticks in their hands, they crouched down beside the tall chimney-like termite heap and poked several holes in the sand into which water was trickled from a *gourd*. I watched as they stirred together water and clay, slapping the mud mixture on top of each hole. They beat two sticks together rapidly on top of a third stick on the ground—faster and faster—tapping until Jillo finally took off the mud lid and out came a swarm of winged termites. Squealing excitedly, the boys pounced on them, tearing off heads and squishing wriggling bodies into their mouths.

Some of the other boys dug out a small mound with long sticks and found the biggest maggot I'd ever seen. Ignoring my screwed-up face, they insisted on giving me the revolting white worm as an offering.

Wondering what the noise was all about, Gabbra came over to investigate. "Look what the boys have given me," I said, holding the squirming maggot gingerly in the palm of my hand.

"That's the prized queen termite—she's huge!" exclaimed Gabbra. "When the boys pound the ground with their sticks they're tricking the termites by pretending the rains have come. I'll eat the queen if you don't want it."

Gabbra bit into the maggot. "It's full of good protein. Mmmmm! Creamy like peanut butter," she laughed, while I made a gagging sound.

"Come, we'll look inside a termite hill." Gabbra scraped off a section of the chimney. A system of tunnels spread out along a miniature community centre.

"See the air holes? That's how the heat escapes. The whole thing is made by millions of clever termite workers," she said. "Sometimes they build the hills up to twenty feet high."

Gabbra left the boys dining on their banquet of bugs to return to her duties and I stayed, photographing them as they played. To my amazement, they approached one of the camels and washed their hands and faces in its urine.

Gulping back a feeling of nausea at this strange behaviour, I sat on a rock for a moment. I watched as they held out their skinny arms in a straight line and ran around, making low throaty droning voices. I realized they were probably imitating a fleet of planes whirling in the sky. They would have seen me flying just above the *manyatta* before landing.

An idea hit me like a sledge hammer to the head. "*That's it!*" I cried out loud. "*Jillo, you're a genius!*" I knew I had to get back to Dad's plane.

Pulling Jillo by the hand, I caught up to Gabbra. "Will you please tell Jillo to take me to the plane?" I asked excitedly.

Her questioning eyes opened wide for a moment, then she grinned. "Of course! The medical kit?" she whispered.

I nodded.

Gabbra explained the situation carefully to

Jillo, and I had to run to catch up with him as he headed toward the tethered camels. He packed two *shukas* and a *gourd* filled with milk onto one side of the camel, his spear on the other. Then he pulled me up behind him.

It was so hot that I reached down and fished out one of the *shukas* to cover my head. I knew we were on the right track because I recognized the place where I'd photographed the Streizman's bush crow, and the enormous tree that held twenty baboons.

At one stage, Jillo turned around to face me. His eyes were wide with fear. I knew we must be travelling through the Plain of Darkness because he had our camel going at a gallop. I patted his back to reassure him.

There, beside the clump of cactus and desert roses was the same dust-covered Acacia tree we sat under when we drank tea with Chief Jallaba. I glanced up quickly at the huge white termite hill, looking for the deadly spitting cobra. It must have found another 'castle' to invade.

We trudged up hill and down again, passing familiar-looking termite towers. The camel never faltered, trekking at a steady pace for an hour, stepping carefully over rocks and boulders, until I could see the tip of the plane on the bushy airstrip.

When we arrived, Jillo drank from the *gourd* before passing it to me—warm and frothy, heavy and a bit sour. Camel's milk never tasted as good as it did at that moment. Then he tethered the camel to an Acacia tree, where it flopped down on its elbows.

I didn't see the giant thorny stick insect until Jillo poked it with his finger. It was a foot long, with black beady eyes and feelers that moved around on top of its head. It blended in beautifully with the thin dry branch it was resting on. I took several pictures, knowing that back at home my photo of this awesome bug would look terrific enlarged fifty times on a giant screen.

The plane's key hung off the oil dipstick under the engine cowling, just where Dad left it.

"Found it, Jillo!" I yelled to him, waving the key in the air. Seeing my enthusiasm, he jumped up and down in anticipation.

I unlocked the cabin door and opened the little window while he climbed up beside me.

"Come on, I'll take you for a ride, but only on the ground because Dad would get mad at me if I took the plane up." I did a quick routine walk-around inspection and checked the tire pressure.

"Hey, Jillo, I'm looking to see that there aren't any birds' nests or snakes in the engine cowling!" I joked, but it fell on deaf ears. I pushed him over to the other side, fastened our seat belts and turned the key.

Because the plane had been sitting idle for a while, I was happy that the propeller spun over.

Placing my feet on the steering pedals, I turned the plane around and guided it down the runway. As we bumped along the rough ground, Jillo clapped his hands, slapped his thighs and roared with laughter. I loved an appreciative audience.

We did one or two lengths of the runway and then returned to the same spot where I'd landed the plane with Dad. "That's the end of the ride, Borana-boy. Let's go home," I said

Reaching behind the passenger seat for the emergency First Aid kit, I found everything Gabbra might need: sutures, needles, sterile gauze, antibiotic ointment, Tetanus vaccine and extra-strength Tylenol. It was enough to treat all the wounded men back at the *manyatta*.

I knew Jillo would be fascinated with all this First Aid stuff. I locked the door, but before I could hang the key back on the oil dipstick—my usual routine—Jillo distracted me, clamouring to get at my medical treasure-box.

Setting the key down temporarily on the step, I opened the box to keep him quiet. I showed him the sutures and needles and pretended to sew two pieces of my skin together, pulling imaginary thread up into the air and back into my arm. He looked blankly at me. He probably didn't understand what on earth I was doing.

"I'm stitching up a pretend wound, can't you see?" I said, rather annoyed. I jabbed my arm with the other finger and he nodded politely, grinning at me as though I was utterly mad.

"Oh, never mind! Take me back to Gabbra," I muttered. "At least the kids back home are a more appreciative lot."

Feeling irritated, I marched off with the precious medical kit under my arm in the direction of the camel, leaving Jillo to run after me.

I remembered Nagya telling me camels must not travel at night because it's too cold for them, and now we only had an hour to go before dusk. I looked back and there was no sign of the Borana boy. I began to feel anxious.

When my anxiety turned to panic, I decided to go back to the plane and look for Jillo. I untethered the camel and prodded its front feet with my stick. It immediately lifted its rear end, then the front. Proud of my new driving skills, I guided the obedient camel by the nose back to the runway, talking to it like the herds boys did, and decided my new pet should be called Clarence.

Jillo stood on top of the plane with his arms outstretched, roaring like he did back at the *manyatta*. He must have climbed the step onto the strut, scrambled along the wing and somehow hauled himself up to the roof.

"What are you *doing*?" I yelled angrily. "Get down, *right now*!"

He turned around and stared at me with his mouth open. Then his arms collapsed beside him and he looked very sad. It dawned on me he probably thought the plane would take off if he raised his arms and roared like a Cessna.

When I beckoned, he slid down and landed in soft sand. Grabbing the stick from me, he tapped the camel's feet bringing it to sitting position, and we both clambered on.

Moaning and slobbering, Clarence galloped all the way back through the Dida Galgalu Plains, past the baboon tree and the desert rose bushes, into the safety of the *manyatta*.

Clarence.

Chapter 8

BLOOD, DUNG AND BRAINSQUEEZING

USING THE MEDICATION that I brought from the plane, Gabbra and the women nursed the surviving men back to health and, after mourning the loss of our fourth brave warrior, everyone returned quietly to their chores.

When I told Gabbra that I was beginning to feel rather weak from too much sun, she handed me a *gourd* of water and said it was also from lack of food.

I witnessed two warriors forcing a camel to kneel down on its elbows. One warrior tied a leather thong around the camel's neck, causing the jugular vein to bulge.

"Riley, this may shock you," said Gabbra, "but what you are about to see is normal practice around here. There's a reason why I'm showing you what happens."

To my horror, the other tribesman shot an arrow into the vein from close range. The blood began pumping in great spurts into a *gourd* he was holding.

"Gabbra, I think I'm going to throw up," I quavered.

Ignoring me, she said, "Look, the blood will now be mixed with milk. Understand, Riley, we survive on this diet, especially in the temporary drought situation we're in right now."

I began to feel light-headed. She caught my arm as I swayed backwards and said calmly, "My friend, you will have to drink blood and milk from this camel or you will die."

After a few days I managed to keep the blood/milk mixture down without vomiting and felt surprisingly strong and energetic.

One morning, Jillo and his gang of young herding boys took on the duty of leading the camels at sunup to Dumbuluk Well and, together with the girls, returned by sundown with a supply of fresh water.

Gabbra warned me I must start helping with chores around the *manyatta,* and I dreaded that moment. I knew she was watching me as I sat outside the çamel pen. Out of the corner of my eye, I could see her waiting for me to finish my journal so I kept busy, writing, sketching and taking photos.

Fascinated, I studied a horned dung beetle using its head to push a small ball of camel dung—five times the size of the beetle—across the path to the other side.

With my camera I captured nursing mothers and naked children playing in the sand. I photographed the faces of wounded warriors and tribesmen, and boys tending camels. I took pictures of wrinkled old men and women drinking tea, and portraits of Gabbra with her slender arms around Nagya and Ayasha. Sketches here, photographs there—wow!—what a slide presentation I'd give back home! I knew my high school friends would be fascinated.

With photo journalism in my blood, I became obsessed with these amazing people; their lifestyle, their culture, and most of all, their fierce passion to help one another. But, could the vanishing Boranas of Dumbuluk continue to survive the drought? Was there something I could do to make people back home aware of their problem? If I did, would I be interfering with a culture that had survived hundreds of years of famine, drought and bandit attacks? I recalled my mother's words, *"...It's important that you help change the world and make a difference..."*

My thoughts were interrupted by Gabbra standing beside me.

"Riley, I have something to tell you which you will not like very much. I'm warning you not to take any more pictures of my tribe."

"What are you talking about? I'll never get another chance, Gabbra. *Film is cheap—opportunity rare.* That's what Mom used to..."

"They believe you are stealing their souls into what they call the *Evil Black Box* and it's upsetting them," she interrupted me. "I have tried to explain to them, but they are not happy."

I was stunned. "Well I'll use the telephoto lens so they don't know I'm photographing them."

"I understand what you're saying Riley, but they must not be aware. Anyway, it's your turn to milk the camel," said Gabbra. She took my arm firmly and guided me to where the camels were tethered.

"First I will teach you how to make a fire, and then I shall show you how to wash the camels' nipples," she said, catching me frowning with disapproval at a child sucking milk from one of the camel's teats.

"Yuck! I'm not doing that!" I exclaimed indignantly. "I'd rather take those fat-tailed sheep for a walk instead."

"That's boys' work. Now bring some dung and sticks for the fire," said Gabbra, laughing at me.

Hating every moment but learning quickly, I set light to a mound of camel dung for fuel and poured water for boiling into an aluminum pot. I spilled water from the *kibuyu* when I tried to carry it on top of my head like the other girls.

"I'm not made out to do this type of work," I complained as Gabbra coaxed me into washing a toddler's dirty behind with some of the warm water I'd saved.

"Here is my camel, handle her with care," said Gabbra, ignoring my whining. "Our camels are usually docile, but be warned, they kick fiercely and are frightened of strangers, unless you know how to sing to them."

When I tripped clumsily over the female camel's big floppy foot, the beast's one eye glared down at me—a menacing and mean-looking black eye surrounded by a double fringe of long eyelashes. As I stared at the animal's face, the tufts of hair that stuck out all the way down her long neck began to shake and she bawled, baring her big teeth at me.

Seeing the effect I had on this camel, Gabbra came to my side quickly, singing sweetly until the animal calmed down.

Still quaking with fear I announced, "Gabbra, I will *not* milk this stupid animal," and turned my back on her.

She caught my arm. "One day, I *know* you will milk that camel, Riley."

Nagya's strength returned, and his wounds healed. Gabbra and I spoke quietly together while he rested on a bed of camel skins outside his hut.

"Riley, you have saved Nagya's life and many of his warriors with the tetanus vaccine and antibiotics. I was beginning to give up hope," she said, with a look of relief. "What a brainwave you had! I didn't think of the medical box on the plane."

Gabbra was happy. This was the chance I was waiting for and I nudged her arm gently. "You promised to teach me your song and I want you to explain every word in English. Please could we do it now?"

She nodded and knelt in front of me. "In my language, I'm sending grateful thanks to heaven and earth for giving us water and camels in this time of drought. I'm asking for rain, continued health, and survival of our tribe. I'm also praising our mother, especially, and asking her forgiveness for any wrongdoing. I'm grateful to Kallu our spiritual Elder for his wisdom and lastly, thankful for being chosen to sing praises at the bottom of Dumbuluk well. Now, watch my lips and repeat every word I say."

I attempted the first line, collapsing into giggles because Gabbra tried hard to keep a straight face. Obviously amused, Nagya covered his mouth with one hand and snorted, his eyes drawn into narrow slits.

"You're laughing at me, aren't you?" I said, grinning up at him. It was difficult from that moment on to take my singing lesson seriously, but I learned Gabbra's song, line by line, until I could chant it in the *Galla* language. Of course, I could never sing it like her, but it was an accomplishment for me.

The sun sank slowly, painting our skins a glowing bronze, and I was content to sit with Nagya and Gabbra beside a big communal fire, far from the milking camels. Nagya covered my head and shoulders with his red-striped *shuka* for warmth.

"Grey smoke from this lump of camel dung might bother you, Riley, but it keeps mosquitoes away," murmured Gabbra, as Nagya lit the offensive dung heap and threw it beside the fire.

"You have done well today," she said, smiling at me. "We have to fetch water from the well at daybreak tomorrow. Nagya, do you feel healthy enough?"

"Yes, nurse, I *will* be fit to go," said Nagya,

firmly. "Now, let's change the subject. It's brainstorm time! I feel like talking about our plans for the future as I promised. You go first, Gabbra."

She opened her mouth to speak, but hesitated. I knew she might have difficulty explaining her confused feelings to Nagya. I wondered if she had told him about Sam.

"I cannot reverse what I have already learned in Canada," Gabbra said. "Nagya, I have to tell you something. I've fallen in love."

Nagya's mood changed abruptly. I noticed his hands were shaking. A terrible silence hung over us. Nagya looked into his sister's eyes and spoke quietly to her in the *Galla* language.

"I know what you're thinking, Nagya," continued Gabbra after he spoke to her. "I'm really bothered by the promise I gave to our mother, but I know she would understand my decision to not keep the tribal tradition. I will *not* marry a Borana man and live the nonintellectual life of a humble tribal woman. I want to choose my own husband." Then she said quietly, "Sam is the son of a Somali diplomat…"

"*He's Somali?*" Nagya spluttered. I'd never seen him so angry. "My own sister is in love with a Somali *Shifta*… "

"Brother," said Gabbra, quietly, "please don't be so hurt and angry. Even though he was born in Somalia, Sam has nothing to do with that clan of bandits. His father is the Somali ambassador in Vancouver. Sam's had the same education as you, except he's in university right now."

"I guess you're old enough to make your own decisions," he muttered.

Nagya turned his back on us, but she gently pulled him round to face her. "Please listen to me, Nagya. What if *you* fell in love with a girl from another tribe? You know yourself that in Canada they have no rigid rules or culture like we do here. You're free to think, behave and believe—within reason of course. And I love Sam with all my heart."

All these years I watched my secretive, quiet friend studying hard, walking my dog, behaving like the perfect student. She told me it was her destiny to keep her mother's promise to teach Borana tribal culture, yet Nagya—although he knew she was too westernized to live in Dumbuluk—was obviously shocked with Gabbra's stunning confession.

"That news will take some time to sink in, Gabbra," Nagya said. "What are *your* plans, Riley-girl? What will you do when you go back to Vancouver?"

"I'm going to make plans to return some day to study more of your culture," I said. "You've taught me so much, but I still don't quite understand the duties of a Borana woman. Honestly, I'm getting the idea but I'll be gone before it's my turn to milk a smelly camel." I grinned at Nagya.

Gabbra smiled at her brother as their eyes met briefly.

"There's more," I continued. "Visualize me as a travelling photo journalist, educating the world with my exotic pictures and editorials of vanishing tribes. I'll have my own fundraising organization…"

Gabbra interrupted me. "You see, Nagya, she's obviously not going to get married and have children immediately after she graduates. She won't be tied down but when she does marry, it will have to be someone who can tame her," she laughed.

Before I could protest, Nagya said, "You don't seem to realize, Riley, that women are very valuable in our culture. They get snapped up fast before they're fourteen, without argument or protest."

"He means that a woman's future husband pays a dowry of many camels to her father," explained Gabbra.

"He has to pay up before he can get married?" I asked. "Hmmm. Sounds similar, but not with livestock. When a girl gets engaged back home, the guy might present her with a ring, but it's usually the girl's parents who pay for their daughter's wedding, although that's changing too."

I could see Nagya grinning at me. "I'd throw in ten more camels, five chickens and two fat-tailed sheep for a ..."

"Tell her about the behaviour strap, Nagya," said Gabbra, punching her brother playfully on the arm.

If Nagya was still angry with Gabbra about her Somali boyfriend, he did not show it. "A newly-married woman wears a fertility pouch around her neck," he said. "Oh, I forgot to mention, there's a four-foot-long leather strap tied around her neck which hangs down the back."

"What's the strap for?" I asked.

"It's like a halter."

"What do you mean?" I was suspicious.

"Well," he looked at me sideways, "the husband pulls the strap to keep his new wild and frisky wife in order until she's tamed," he said, beaming at me.

"Get serious," I said.

"*Now* I'll be serious," announced Nagya. "I have an idea. It came to me in a dream as I lay weak and feverish in my cot. It's time for the Borana tribe to have a lifestyle change. My dream is to train as a pilot in Vancouver, then return to Kenya, as I told you. I intend to buy a small plane and fly to remote areas south of the Sahara. Gabbra, I, too, cannot reverse the Western education I've had, and I've made Father understand I will not be taking over the chief's position."

Surprised, Gabbra stared at him, but said nothing.

"Eventually, I'll buy a bus that will take young boys *and girls* to the local mission school on a weekly basis," he continued. "I know the missionaries will pay for transportation and a driver if we help them build a dormitory where the children can sleep. In exchange, we'll bring a weekly supply of water," said Nagya. "The first group of kids could go to school alternating with the second group that stays behind to herd camels and fetch water. Like taking turns at Dumbuluk Well," he explained.

"I guess you're saying that herding camels and water supply would be taken care of at all times, but *every* child would have an education," I said.

Nagya told us he also dreamed of a long underground pipe leading from the well to the *manyatta,* with water being piped into a huge holding tank.

"Wouldn't that upset the balance and way of life for nomadic tribes?" I asked.

Nagya laughed out loud. "That's what the Elders will say, but we would need fewer camels if water was close by. Now, if half the camels were sold for seed, we could plant pastures and buy cattle and more sheep and goats," he said. "We wouldn't have to move very far at all."

Gabbra said, softly, "Our nomadic culture has been handed down for hundreds of years, and that's the way they've always been. Perhaps you're right, Nagya. If we are to survive, it's time to change. Oh, and how would we irrigate the pasture?"

I reminded her about the portable irrigation lines we had seen on farms in the Okanagan Valley, when we took a trip outside of Vancouver last summer.

"Yes, but how would we build a pipeline?" Gabbra pointed out. "Who can dig such a long tunnel, and how could we afford a tank and then all this irrigation equipment?" She always asked the most practical questions.

"Ask Riley's dad," said Nagya. "*He's* the expert!"

Sitting together, we gazed up at a dark navy-blue sky studded with a million diamond stars that were clearer than I had ever seen. I realized that back home, most of the galaxy was obscured by high-rise buildings and bright city lights.

One twinkling star stood out brighter than the rest—I knew Mom was out there watching over me. Thinking of my mother reminded me also of Dad. It seemed ages since he and the Chief had left, yet it was just ten days ago, and I'd seen and done so much. I had new respect and tender feelings for Gabbra; and more than that for Nagya.

Flames from the fire illuminated our faces and a feeling of sheer happiness engulfed me.

Something stirred close by in the shadows. I turned and saw a solitary figure standing stiffly behind me. Ayasha had been there all the time during our private brainstorming. Although she could not understand our conversation, I felt chilled by her frosty, silent presence.

Nagya spoke to Ayasha and, pulling her gently by the hand, allowed her to sit close together between him and Gabbra.

This strange girl tormented me. Verging on a hissy fit, I felt my temper rising like molten lava. Trembling with anger—or was it jealousy?—I stared into the dying embers of the fire, imagining frantic flames licking the air like snakes' tongues. Dry Acacia branches creaked and bent in the night breeze like the wicked, cackling witches waving their arms wildly over the cauldron in Shakespeare's *Macbeth*.

"Why is *she* always here?" I finally burst out. "Everywhere I turn, I see her looking at me!"

Nagya and Gabbra exchanged glances.

Nagya opened his mouth to speak but, without waiting for an explanation, I ran to my hut, burning-hot tears scalding my ice-cold cheeks.

Chapter 9

THE DIAMOND NOSE STUD

I SLEPT FITFULLY in my hard, lumpy bed beside Gabbra. Hyenas snuffled and laughed like lunatics in the distance, while women in huts beside us snored and ground their teeth. Hurt, anger and resentment wounded my rearranged feelings. I was crazy with jealousy knowing that Ayasha and Nagya were sitting close together by the fire.

Was Nagya just having a warm flirtation with

both Ayasha and me? Maybe it was just a schoolgirl infatuation that would end when Dad returned to take me home. Then why, I reasoned with myself, did my gut feeling indicate we had a strong attraction for one another?

The moon was full—an enormous spotlight aimed at my face through a large hole in the camel-hide wall—almost prompting me to think these volatile thoughts. Pulling the camel skin blanket around my shoulders, I sat up and hugged my knees, staring at the hypnotic yellow 'eye'. I needed an adventure and I knew exactly what to do. Didn't I promise myself I'd climb down to the bottom of Dumbuluk Well?

I'd surprise Gabbra and Nagya by leaving earlier than normal and get there ahead of them. I could sing Gabbra's song, purify the water and start hauling water like a Borana girl.

Although it was dark at six a.m., I could still see where the camels were tethered in the glow of the dying fire. I crept quietly over to the animals and recognized the male I'd named Clarence—the one Jillo and I rode to the plane.

Stepping over his scrawny, rope-like tail, I shoved a water container into the grass straps on one side of the beast and my backpack containing Nagya's *shuka,* camera and a *gourd* of blood and milk in case of hunger, on the other side.

As I untied the leather strap around Clarence's legs he began to moan and grunt. I sang Gabbra's song quietly to calm him down, then, hitching my skirt above my thighs, I stepped onto his shoulder. Pulling myself up by a tuft of scraggly hair on the camel's hump, I sat with my legs astride his back and leaned forward so that I could tap his feet with my stick.

When Clarence heaved himself up, I looked behind to see if anyone was following. A lone figure, vaguely recognizable from the dim firelight, stood in the doorway of a hut, staring in my direction. Always watching, Ayasha, always watching. Did she ever sleep?

Shivering in the early morning breeze, I pulled Nagya's red *shuka* from my bag to wrap around my shoulders, but it slipped to the ground as we moved off through the thorny entrance of the *manyatta*. I left it lying there and concentrated instead on prodding my camel to keep him moving. When the first ray of light crept over the hills, I knew it meant only one more hour to the well.

Busy birds chattered loudly and crickets sang their deafening sound, but the sun, now warm on my face, forced me to think happier thoughts. I reminisced on my adventures over the last several days: hair and dress makeover, frightening *Shifta* attack, smelly little boy down the tunnel, death, how brave Gabbra was, Nagya's wounds, 'jumping' Jillo, evil Ayasha, blood and milk diet, maggots, and the fascinating lifestyle of Borana people.

As Clarence plodded along the familiar track toward the well, I began to feel proud and exhilarated because I'd managed to control the animal without help. I smiled to myself as I fished for my camera in the backpack. It was so beautiful and peaceful in this savannah of stubby yellowing grass. Trees and bushes were covered with dust, and boulders looked like the round backs of grey elephants.

A brilliant pink-legged ostrich raced along beside us, blazing a chalk-white trail across the barren scrubland. I remember Nagya saying that if a male ostrich's legs were blushing, it must be the mating season.

Looking down from the top of the hill, I could see the hedge of thorns which surrounded Dumbuluk well.

Suddenly, two tiny, light-grey antelopes—called dikdiks—skittered quickly from bush to bush, kicking up tiny puffs of powdery dust where they landed on the track in front of me. Wondering what disturbed these terrified little creatures, I focused on a shaking sandy-covered bush and drew my breath in sharply. Staring at us through the branches was a dirty-yellow, scrawny-looking lion, crouching, waiting to pounce.

Spooked, my camel reared and pawed the ground, bawling loudly while the king of beasts got up and sauntered weakly away from us, probably avoiding a dangerous confrontation with a camel notoriously stronger than himself. He lost out on a mid-morning snack—me or the dikdiks.

I screamed in terror as Clarence broke into a faster gait, legs stretched out so high that his feet slapped hard against his long neck. Tears dribbled down my face as I bounced up and down and flopped from side to side on my stomach.

I shouldn't be here alone...why was I so stupid?

What was it Nagya tried to teach me? When you lead the camel down to the well, prod it with a stick and speak softly. But first you have to get *off* the camel! In my panic I couldn't remember how to make the galloping maniac stop so I kicked him hard with my feet.

"Stop! Please stop!" I shouted, clinging tightly to Clarence's strong bony neck. The stubborn camel sailed like a galleon in rough seas, never pausing.

At last, he trotted down to the well and halted at the mud-and-stick trough. He stopped so abruptly that I found myself swinging upside down under his neck, landing with a heavy thud onto the sand. The leather pouch around my neck tore off the aluminum-beaded necklace as I fell, and both nose stud and little clay camel spilled out.

Clarence bore down, with jaws stretched open to get a piece of me. He raised both front legs and repeatedly stomped and pounded the sand with his big feet, just missing my camera and the backpack. I clambered over the trough and stood on the muddy lip of the well, yelling hysterically at him. Obviously angry, he swung his head like a sledge hammer to try and destroy me, his fierce teeth snapping and biting.

Again, Clarence reared up menacingly, lunging with his massive front legs. As I tried to get to the other side of the well, he lobbed a slimy spitball at my head and lollopped off into the bush.

Tears of rage flowed down my camel-slimed face as I tried to wipe off the offensive spit with the back of my hand. I was bruised, insulted and nauseous. Vision blurred, I missed my step and fell, slipping and sliding into the hole. Grabbing blindly at branches of the ladder that the Borana singers had made, I hit my head on a rock jutting out from the side, and tumbled helplessly down the well.

Floundering in fresh spring water, I saw in the eerie half-light my waterlogged halo of braids floating above me, and flashes of white exploded inside my head. I felt I was being whisked down long, dark pipes, swirling round and round in the water and I could hear Gabbra singing from far away. Water gushed, fast and furious, and braided snakes seemed to squeeze me tightly around the neck.

I was drowning.
Blackness.
Nothingness.

Strong arms clasped me tightly as I rocked gently from side to side. I sensed a pungent smell of camel and someone stroking my hair.

"How are you feeling, Riley-girl?"

Struggling to focus my eyes, I gazed into the dark smouldering eyes of Nagya, the warrior.

"Am I alive? How did you find me?" I murmured.

"Don't talk any more," he said softly, cushioning my head against his chest. "Close your eyes. We're riding back to the *manyatta* on my camel. You are a special gift from the Heavens and, yes, you *are* alive." I succumbed to exhaustion and relaxed, cradled in Nagya's arms.

Despite the hot noon sun, my teeth chattered as though I had been pulled out of a frozen pond. I was still in shock, shivering and trembling under the blanket. We plodded along at a steady rate while I was lulled into a deep sleep. When I awoke, Nagya was singing Gabbra's song.

"That song makes me happy," I said.

After what seemed an eternity, I asked again, "How did you find me, Nagya?"

"A warrior night-guard woke me before day-break and said he suspected the bandits had stolen a camel. He ran from his lookout point in time to see a camel racing down the track with someone on it," he explained.

"Ayasha found a red *shuka* lying in the sand and brought it to me. It was the one I had thrown over your shoulders, and I became afraid. I thought the *Shifta* had captured you," he said.

His voice was husky and shaking. I'd never heard him sound so emotional before and I instinctively put my arms around his waist.

"I roused Gabbra and told her to keep watch over the women and children," he continued. "My men went from hut to hut, and when we were satisfied no strangers were lurking, I took my camel and followed fresh tracks out of the *manyatta*. I knew then the camel was not going toward the Somali border, but had taken the path to the well.

"It was still cold when I left—not more than an hour after you'd gone. Remember, camels can catch chills in the early morning air if they are made to run and sweat, so I covered my camel with a blanket and rested for awhile," explained Nagya. "When I felt the first warm rays of sun, I proceeded."

Nagya said that tracks stopped at the well but it looked like there had been a scuffle, and he was about to go on when he saw a tiny object shining brightly beside pieces of clay in the sand.

"I bent down and picked up a diamond nose

stud. I remembered you opening your leather pouch and showing me the stud and my clay camel when you first arrived here. I knew you must be somewhere close," Nagya said. "My first thought was to climb down the well and there, in the half-light, I saw you lying like a ghost. Your hair floated out around you and only your face was above water. I thought you were dead," he said in a cracked voice.

"You were unconscious so I resuscitated you. I sang Gabbra's song to see if you would respond, carrying you over my shoulder all the way up the ladder. It was not until I wrapped you tightly in the blanket and cradled you in my arms that you opened your eyes. I was very relieved, Riley-girl," he said.

We returned to the *manyatta* at high noon to find Gabbra waiting for us at the entrance.

"I was so worried about you," she said in a wavering voice as Nagya carried me into the hut and laid me down on the cot. "Thank you, brother, for finding my friend. I thought *they* had taken her away. Now Riley must rest," she said, holding my hand.

"It was a miracle," Nagya said. "That magic nose stud seemed to wink at me." He backed slowly out of the hut. "I must soothe your bawling camel, Riley. He's stressed and chilled and badly scratched from running through thorn bushes."

I didn't feel like telling Nagya and Gabbra the reason for my impulsive adventure. Perhaps they knew.

I woke up feeling better. Then Gabbra told me she had sat beside me for two days and nights.

"I was watching for any sign of trauma, checking your pulse and mopping your forehead as you went in and out of sleep," she said.

I heard a familiar, but anxious, voice at the entrance of the hut.

"I want to see my Little Red Fox!" My father had returned from his two-week assignment with the Chief.

I sat up, blinked and looked around. "Daddy, please take me home."

Early the next day, Chief Jallaba helped Gabbra, Nagya, Dad and me load up the LandRover with our belongings, including my backpack and camera which Nagya had found beside the well.

We were heading home with the added benefit of Nagya joining us! Gabbra and I would return to high school in Vancouver's West End, Dad had to report to headquarters, and Nagya was enrolled at flight training school.

"Ah!" announced Nagya as he climbed into the front seat beside both fathers. "I see you've changed out of your tribal clothes, white Riley-girl."

I smiled cockily at him because he also wore shorts and t-shirt. My hair was threaded through the back of my ball-cap, and my mother's diamond nose stud nestled in its proper place.

To my delight, Jillo hopped into the LandRover beside me. He gawked at my shorts and top and pawed my bare knees with his grubby hands.

I had forgotten how uncomfortable the trip was to the airstrip. While I did the walk-around inspection of the plane, Nagya followed me every step of the way, even climbing with me onto the wheel and up the struts to the top of the wing.

"What do you do now?" asked Nagya, knowing full well what the routine was. He probably didn't believe I could actually fly this plane, and he was testing me.

"Here, hold the nozzle into the fuel tank while I wobble this hand pump back and forth," I said. Our fuel was pumped from a large tank which the Chief said was filled twice a year by the government survey team from Nairobi. Nagya watched me as I inspected the fuel by putting the stem of a glass beaker under the wing and holding it up to the light to check for contamination.

"I'm impressed. Pretty efficient at this, aren't you?" he said.

I heard Dad bellowing with frustration. "Riley, where did you put the key? I've spent twenty minutes searching for it."

Startled by my father's anger, I stopped what I was doing and thought very hard. What had I done with that key? My mind drew a blank. The high midday sun seemed to glare accusingly at me. I began to explain quickly to Dad about taking Jillo for a ride in the plane, and how I was distracted by his clamouring to see what was in the medical box. Instinctively, I turned to look at that funny jumping boy.

"I remember putting it…" and stopped mid-sentence. As the sun glinted on a familiar shiny object nestling firmly in Jillo's torn ear-lobe, the truth struck me like a bolt of lightning. I recalled leaving the key on the step of the plane. Jillo had distracted me and I'd forgotten to hang it under the engine cowling.

"Dad! The key! There it is!" I shouted and my father stared at me as if I had gone mad. "Jillo, you clever boy—you *did* take care of me!" I hugged the shocked little camel-herder until we both lost our balance and fell into a pile of soft sand.

"There's no safer place to keep stolen treasure," chuckled Nagya, hauling me up by one arm.

Perhaps Jillo's torn ear lobe wasn't such a ridiculous place to wedge the plane key. It reminded me of the time Dad and I visited Tanzania years ago, when we had seen an old man walking along the road with a bundle of sticks on his back. This wrinkled man used the stretched hole in his ear lobes to hold a few groceries: he had pushed a can of baked beans into one earlobe, and threaded a nine-volt battery through the other.

My father revved up the engine, startling a huge black hornbill perched in a nearby Acacia tree. It was so close that I could see its long eyelashes and scarlet lipstick-red horned beak— definitely a female.

Dad turned to me. "Well, Miss Mechanic, at least you won't have to hot-wire this Cessna to get it started. I forgive you for being so absent-minded about the key, and you can make up for it by showing me your journal and doing a presentation for headquarters when we get home."

He took the plane up above the savannah, heading it toward Nairobi, where we would eventually board a flight home to Canada.

From my little window I could see a cloud of dust snaking its way through the Dida Galgalu Plain of Darkness—the Chief and Jillo were going home to Dumbuluk. I studied the back of Nagya's kinky black hair and found myself thinking of Ayasha. I looked for her before leaving the *manyatta,* but this time she was nowhere to be seen.

I could hardly wait to tell friends back at

school about my bizarre experiences during spring
break in Africa.

.

Dikdiks. (pic: Margaret Hayes)

Chapter 10

HOT AIR BALLOON

NAGYA MOVED TO THE FLYING
SCHOOL soon after we returned to Vancouver,
while Gabbra and I plunged back into school.

As the weeks passed, I found that Nagya was
on my mind all the time so I immersed myself in
the most challenging goal I had ever attempted.
Guided by sheer determination, I formulated a
fundraising plan to build a water pipeline for
Dumbuluk! I would create a speech and multi-

media presentation illustrating the nomadic lifestyle of the Borana and the desolation caused by the past two years of drought.

Late one evening I found Gabbra buried in a sea of textbooks. I told her about my plan and she said I was crazy, but I knew it could work.

"Nothing stands in your way once you've made up your mind, Riley, but how will you find enough money for this ambitious plan?" she said.

"I didn't earn the nickname of 'Red Robin Hood Riley' for nothing, you know," I said, shaking the back of her chair teasingly. I told Gabbra that, after all, I'd been using my notorious powers of persuasion all my life, and I was confident.

On Saturday morning I had a call from the photography shop that my photo slides were developed. Dad and I picked them up immediately. The camera salesman asked why I didn't use a digital camera. He laughed when we told him that without power in the desert, rechargeable batteries would be useless.

Dad insisted I practise my show-and-tell in his office. "Nobody will be there to disturb us because it's a weekend," he said. "Just skeleton staff."

After we loaded the projector, I closed the drapes of the board room, switched off the lights and stared expectantly at the giant screen on the wall. I had portraits of Jillo and his friends, the warriors, the Elders and the women of the village, and girls carrying pots of water on their heads. There were some fantastic shots of miniature antelopes and Streizman's bush crow, the huge stick insect with its bulbous eyes, and three camels slurping water at the well—all much larger on the screen.

Clicking through the next several slides, I paused in bewilderment at the group photos of Nagya, Gabbra and Ayasha. I could see Gabbra's arms clearly around the other two, but her face wasn't there. It hovered as a mysterious pale circle beside theirs in every single picture. It didn't make sense, I reasoned with myself. To make sure Gabbra's head was not obliterated from any more photos, I clicked on, feverishly, stopping at a picture of her alone. Determined to get a closer look, I strode up to the projection on the wall, wiping my clammy-feeling hands down the front of my shirt. I recalled taking this photo of her as she ran down the hill toward me, her arms outstretched.

Up on the wall of that silent boardroom, Gabbra's faceless figure stood on the top of the hill, poised in imminent flight.

"I'm puzzled," I said to my father. "Look. Gabbra has a body but no head in every single picture of her. What does this mean, Dad?"

Sensing my anguish, Dad left the board room and returned with Mr. Wilson, a professional photographer working for the Agency.

"It's a strange phenomenon," said the photographer, stroking his beard thoughtfully. "Yet I can't explain it in scientific terms. The same thing happened to me several years ago when I took photos of a friend in Montreal. Like an apparition, his face was invisible in every single picture although I could clearly see him standing beside his wife."

He looked at me intently. "It makes my skin crawl to say this, but two weeks later, he was killed in a car accident."

"What are you saying, sir?" I asked, shocked. "Are you suggesting that something might happen to my friend?"

Mr. Wilson laid a hand on my shoulder. "Riley, put it out of your mind," he said kindly. "It's just a weird occurrence. The flash could have been too bright, causing her face to vanish altogether. Perhaps you had your finger in front of the lens. I've done that occasionally in my excitement to snap a good picture."

I could feel anger building up inside from his condescending remarks. First I was going to tell him that I didn't use the flash, and secondly, my fingers were nowhere near the camera lens because I had it on automatic focus, but he and Dad were curious to see the rest of the slides.

Finally, Mr. Wilson got up to leave. "I am

fascinated with your pictures, Riley," he said, sounding genuinely impressed. "I've taken photos of villagers in remote areas of Southern Africa, but yours are incredibly beautiful. I suspect your speech and slides will cause mixed emotions from the audience when they learn how badly northern Kenya is suffering from the drought. Incidentally, I especially like the shot with the kid grinning. What's that delicious-looking white meat he's eating?"

"A juicy maggot," I replied.

"Wow!" he said as he left the room.

Returning to the photo slides of Nagya, Ayasha and the absent Gabbra, I forced myself to believe it was just bad camera luck and put it out of my mind.

Within a month, I was ready to bombard Vancouver with my fundraising project. Dad helped me organize my speeches, even paying for printing costs, refreshments and hall rentals. We opened an account at the bank called "Pipeline for Kenya—The Dumbuluk Account", endorsed by Dad's organization, the International Development & Disaster Agency (IDDA) and finally, we alerted the media. My father was wonderful, and I told him so.

We set up posters in shop windows, school bulletin boards, colleges, universities, and even car windows, with the words:

> # DYNAMIC SPEAKER
> # RILEY FORBES:
>
> # "PIPELINE NEEDED FOR DROUGHT-STRICKEN NOMADS IN KENYA"
>
> ## Photo Presentation
> ## Thursday, 7 p.m.
> ## Admission by donation.

I went down the list of international clubs with donations earmarked for desperate causes, and targeted wealthy celebrities, sharing with them the urgent need of many nations on our planet. My fundraising vision was brought to the attention of a world wildlife foundation, by Mr. Wilson, the photographer who worked in Dad's office. The wildlife directors were curious, and invited me to a private showing in their office. After seeing my photos, they concentrated on the slide of my Streizman's bush crow.

"We have not been successful in

photographing this rare bird at such close range," said one of the directors. "My agency would like to offer you a grant to further study this endangered species, if you are willing to return to northern Kenya. It would feature in our wildlife magazine." I could hardly contain myself as I left the building.

I was exhausted after a month of speeches. Although my plan was to coax money out of older audiences, I was surprised by such enthusiastic applause and generosity from all ages. Due to overwhelming response from radio, television and newspaper coverage, my private school principal insisted I target my largest audience: a lunch-time assembly of high school supporters.

It was the most nerve-wracking speech because I knew almost everyone who came to listen. I stood on the podium, staring at a sea of teenagers, teachers and my principal, and began to shake uncontrollably. *Why now?* I thought, nervously, wiping my soggy hands down the sides of my leather Borana skirt.

I should have felt more confident but my usual bold spirit seemed to have evaporated. Yet, wasn't this the same place I'd debated, campaigned and fought for students' rights all these years? Everyone was expecting the aggressive 'Red Robin Hood Riley' to perform and deliver and here I was, faltering at the start of my speech.

However, as soon as the photo slide show began, I sensed an overpowering awe and inquisitiveness from the audience, and my courage returned.

"Yes, my friends, I have a dream," I said, feeling more comfortable. "A dream to finance a pipeline for the people of Dumbuluk, who have to trek once a week to draw water from the only well in 30 kilometres. These nomadic families are already weakened by drought; there is no pasture left for their livestock and they live in fear of attacks by bandits."

Plans and drawings of the proposed solar-powered water pump for the well were also on display. "Five kilometres of pipe need to be laid, ending in a huge tank of fresh drinking water at a new site for the village of Dumbuluk," I explained.

I told them about Jillo and the camels, the safety tunnel, the bandits, the brave warriors, the boys hunting for termites, and all the dancing and laughter that happen—despite the horror of drought.

"We have the opportunity to help this rapidly vanishing tribe if each student will agree to contribute the price of one day's lunch per week for three months," I said sweetly. "We don't want to destroy their culture but help them adapt in order to survive, and we have to start now before it's too…"

I froze, sucking in my breath sharply, losing all focus on what was supposed to be the most persuasive speech I had ever attempted, and stared at the apparition who invaded my dreams both day and night.

Nagya stood at the back of the hall, grinning at me. He had made the time to come and listen to my speech. We locked eyes. My mind went back to Dumbuluk, the *Shifta* attack, how Nagya nearly died, the camel spitting at me, my near-drowning, and especially the comfort of Nagya's arms while he sang Gabbra's song to me. In those few split seconds I also took in his black suit, white shirt and freshly shaved head. I was so flustered I could not speak.

Someone hissed a warning from below the stage. "Riley Forbes, where are you going with this speech? Get back to the point!"

I gasped. There was an uncomfortable silence from the audience. With difficulty, I tore my eyes away from Nagya's, and struggled to regain my composure.

"Ladies and gentlemen, I want to sum up by telling you that young people have the power to try and save the world. It's time to face new challenges by helping solve one global problem at a time." I swallowed quickly, and looked around at all the familiar faces.

"I see people all over our planet working

together with these same goals. We're all concerned about the threat of climate change, starvation and lack of clean drinking water."

I knew at that precise moment I had them, as it were, eating out of my hands. "I encourage you, as the future caring and powerful generation that you are, to make a difference, and to start with this small village in Kenya. Let's do this together!"

The crowd stood up immediately, whistling, clapping, stamping their feet and chanting my name. Smiling triumphantly, I stepped down from the podium, shook hands with teachers and fellow students, and approached the treasurer's table.

An extremely dark-skinned young man slid a cheque into the donation box. I'd seen him before somewhere. I clicked on 'save' in my brain: *tall, very black, chiseled features, gold ring with lion's head engraving on left hand.*

"Amazing speech, Riley," he was saying. "There is a promising future for Dumbuluk, thanks to you." He squeezed my hand and smiled approvingly at me.

I returned the smile, hoping to find out his name, but he turned and walked quickly toward the exit, leaving behind a waft of cologne that I had smelled before.

I moved slowly through the crowd, looking for

Nagya. At the exit of the high school auditorium, I spotted a small knot of people standing together and heard familiar voices as I drew closer. Dad, Nagya and Chief Jallaba were listening to someone talking. My father promised me he would come to hear my speech, and hoped he would be able to bring Gabbra's father also. The Chief had arrived by plane the day before. They were both attending a series of emergency meetings at IDDA.

"...and she's an activist," said a voice that I recognized. "She starts demonstrations. Give her a reason to fight, and she'll argue it to death until you're beaten, intimidated, submissive. But all the time you think it's her power of gentle persuasion, and you come crawling to her side, smiling and nodding in agreement to anything she says. She took to public speaking and debating, like a duck to water. In short, she's an amazing sixteen-year-old crusader." I recognized the voice of Mr. Daniels, my Vice Principal. When they saw me standing at the door, Dad, Nagya and the Chief chuckled together, and I realized with a prickle of pride they were talking about me.

My father put an arm around my shoulders when I snuggled gratefully up to him.

"She's tiny, but once she's on stage, those green eyes flash and she seems to fill the room, all fired up and enthusiastic," continued Mr. Daniels, "As one of my students put it so aptly—Riley

Forbes has pit-bull tactics, but she's kick-butt good!" They all laughed at me.

I groaned, but Mr. Daniels continued. "Riley, clearly you organized the topic, using reasoning, research and reality. Your appeal was powerful."

Dad turned to me. "I'm so proud of you, my Little Red Fox," he whispered. "I knew you could do it."

A tall woman approached, with her hand outstretched. "Miss Forbes," she said in a deep voice, "I'm a newspaper reporter. We find your story fascinating. You are a young person who has something to say, and I can see why you've been the focus of attention in the media."

I smiled into her eyes, observing a tanned, make-up free face, crew-cut hair and absence of jewelry.

"You are an example of what one teen can accomplish, and I'd like to talk to you," she said, kindly. The reporter took my photograph and scribbled onto a spiral-backed note-pad while I told her the reasons for my campaign. When she had finished asking questions, she leaned forward and whispered in a low voice, "I know your mother very well. Kathleen and I travelled together on the same assignment into Afghanistan. She is a wonderful, powerful person. I see yourself in her—same passionate speaker. She…"

"Forgive me for interrupting, but we have a

table reserved for dinner at the Zanzibar Club on Granville Island," said Chief Jallaba. "Riley, we have much to discuss. Your father, Gabbra and I will wait for you in the car. Nagya will accompany you as soon as you are ready."

At that moment I hated the Chief for disturbing us. After all, the news reporter said she actually knew my mother. She'd watched her laughing; she'd touched her; seen her green eyes sparkling like the brilliant stars that twinkled in Dumbuluk's clear midnight skies. My mouth went dry and I put my hand on the wall to steady myself. I felt a bubble floating uncomfortably inside my throat; a bubble that might either burst with a happy giggle or a sad sob from this fresh reminder of Mom. And she was definitely alive!

When I looked up again, the reporter had left the building.

In a fog-like trance, I headed for the treasurer who was totaling the donations we had collected. He stared at me, apologetically. "It's a lot of money but still not enough. I'm sorry, Riley."

Feeling even more depressed, I sat on the edge of the raised stage and asked myself why I had started this crazy fundraising project in the first place. Memories flashed through my mind: the first meeting with Gabbra and Nagya in Dumbuluk when I was thirteen years old, and returning three years later to a parched land. I had seen from the air a desert graveyard of wild animal skeletons, and learned of Boranas struggling to find enough water for themselves and their camels. If only there was enough money for pump equipment, water pipes and a means of transporting it all to Dumbuluk. I wanted so badly to help this vanishing tribe, but my single-handed efforts didn't seem to be enough.

My eyes prickled with the suggestion of tears when Nagya stood beside me.

"You're upset, Riley-girl," he said, looking concerned.

"I have failed," I said to him, miserably.

"Why? What do you mean?" said Nagya, lifting me up high so that my legs dangled in the air like a limp rag doll. "All I see is success. Everyone loves your ideas. Look at the press! Did you hear the applause?"

His face was out of focus when I peered at him through my tears. "It'll take me months of continuous speeches all over Vancouver to get enough money. I've come up short," I sobbed.

"Well, how much did you figure you'd need?" he said, wiping my wet cheeks gently with the palm of his hand.

"I researched the internet, called pump distributors for details on solar equipment. Then I got in touch with my friend in New York. Her mother works for an international development program with a similar project in the Sudan, and she sent me all the information. I have a little over a third of the total needed for pipes, solar power system, labour, transportation and freight," I explained.

"I can see you have done your homework well. I'm impressed," said Nagya. "Now listen, I'm here to take care of you. We'll sort this money thing out later. Hold my hand, Riley-girl, and let's go to the car and join the others."

I relaxed in the back seat between Nagya and Gabbra. She smelled strongly of cologne, the same scent that was on the guy who donated the cheque at the speech, and I began to wonder if the mystery man I had met earlier was Sam from Somalia.

Nagya laid my hand on his chest. I felt the warmth of his body through his silk shirt and my heart pounded out of control.

"Riley, I shall go myself to the International Development & Disaster Agency and ask them to make up the balance. Be patient. I have learned much from your art of persuasion!" he said, giving me a wink.

"Look at your campaign like a hot air balloon, waiting to be inflated," he said. "People listen to your inspiring and powerful speeches, money starts rolling in because they believe you, and the balloon begins to rise slowly."

"I'm listening, Nagya. I think I know what you're saying," I said.

"Imagine there's a change in the monetary wind. Our balloon is blowing in a different direction than where you originally wanted it to go."

He held my face in his hands. "Success is not beyond your reach, little one. This hot air balloon *will* fly higher than you ever imagined, and I am very proud of you."

The car stopped but I wanted it to drive on and on. I yearned to sit close beside Nagya and savour the moment; to smell his skin, to feel his warm breath on my cheek and hear his words of encouragement.

While the others sauntered into the Zanzibar Club, Nagya caught my arm and pulled me gently out of the car until we stood, alone, on the curb.

He took my hand in his. "I'll tell you what makes me happy. This Borana warrior is in the city, standing beside his red-headed Riley-girl."

Perhaps I was already in that imaginary hot air balloon—floating into dreamland—with Nagya. Our two hearts seemed to speak in riddles, but if I had to share Nagya with Ayasha in Africa, at least I had him all to myself in Canada.

Chapter 11

GOOD VIBES—BAD VIBES

"WELCOME TO THE ZANZIBAR CLUB. My name is Sam and I am your server tonight."

Where had I heard this voice before? Startled, I looked into the twinkling eyes of the tall, extremely dark-skinned man I'd met back at school. He smiled briefly at me, cocked his head to one side and held his hands together, anticipating a drinks order from the Chief. Then I noticed his unusual ring—gold with a lion's head setting. I looked at Gabbra—who was trembling visibly—then quickly back to Sam. That extraordinary smell of cologne was the give-away and it all came together for me. Gabbra had admitted she was in love with Sam, the Somali medical student, when we were down the safety tunnel, and she had given him the ring. He was probably earning extra money waiting tables at night while studying during the day.

When Sam took our order, I saw his arm brush her hair when he passed by and Gabbra, with a fleeting glance at her father, smiled down at her hands.

Nagya leaned over to me and whispered, "I know what you're thinking, white-girl!"

Bringing my thoughts back to what Nagya was insinuating, while nursing the fact that he had not yet met Gabbra's boyfriend, I said, with a quick glance at Sam, "Okay, Nagya the Smart One. Am I thinking that he's doing girl's work by bringing us food and drinks?"

"Exactly!" came the answer.

My father leaned toward me. "The Chief and I have been in deep discussion, and we are impressed with your knowledge of solar-powered equipment."

"Your reasoning was excellent in the presentation we have just heard," said Chief Jallaba, beaming, "and your methods of persuasion I have never before seen in such a young person."

"She's always been comfortable with an audience," said Gabbra, smiling in my direction. She looked different with her hair scraped into a knot at the back. She was more beautiful than I had ever seen her.

"You've changed, Riley," said Gabbra. "You're more quiet and not so impulsive. I remember you used to be a bit of a bully. Nobody dared say 'no' to you. They handed over their money, like everyone else, when you had a good idea for a fundraiser."

"Isn't that a Robin Hood tactic?" piped up Nagya.

Gabbra ignored her brother's comment. "And I remember you pounding your fist on the table to make a point," she continued.

Dad leaned forward again. "Mr. Daniels said you were an effective but menacing pit-bull debater."

His comment seemed to strike a chord of mischief in Nagya. He leaned back in his chair and laughed—a deep belly-laugh that brought tears to his eyes. Beckoning Sam, he said, "Waiter, please bring the young lady your specialty of the evening. Warm camel's milk, isn't it?"

Although both Sam and I knew he was only teasing, I kicked Nagya in the shins, harder than I intended to.

"Oh good. I see you've got your old self

back again," said Nagya, wincing.

The Chief looked serious, as though disapproving of Nagya's behaviour. "Riley, your father and I have something to tell you. It was going to happen anyway, but not as soon as we expected."

My stomach lurched uneasily. With burning face, I stared fearfully at everyone around the table. If this had something to do with Nagya, I didn't want to hear about it. I worried that perhaps Nagya would have to return to Kenya— leaving me in a fluster—not knowing what was going on between him and Ayasha back in Dumbuluk.

Chief Jallaba smiled at me. "Because of your fundraising efforts, the International Development & Disaster Agency has approved this project. It will match the amount you have raised and also make a substantial donation to the Kenyan Government. Riley, let me tell you we have waited a long time for humanitarian aid for northern parts of Kenya. There is a great need of support for food, medical assistance, education and most especially clean water. Young lady, you have done a very great thing for my people," he said.

Surely I was dreaming?

"The Agency has agreed to pay for expertise to assemble the solar equipment," said my father. "The Kenyan government will pay for transportation of all the equipment to Dumbuluk and local experts to assemble the pipes."

After this overwhelming announcement of good news, I could not hide my emotions. Tears of relief began spilling down my cheeks, plopping onto my lap. The fundraiser was going to be a success—I had raised enough money after all. And, better still, Nagya was not going home!

"Wow! Nagya, my dream is coming true. I'm so happy."

I saw Dad wink at Nagya. "You know, I have never seen such a change in personality as in my daughter. A few weeks ago she was spoiled, under-dressed and very rude."

I was hot with embarrassment.

"You were very angry with me," Dad continued. "You said you were bored in the *manyatta* and you were not going to stay for two weeks with a bossy Borana boy to take care of you! I felt very unhappy when I could not find you to say goodbye."

Nagya turned to me with a surprised look on his face. I smiled to myself, thinking how shocked the men must have been when I stepped out of the LandRover: a tiny, flat-chested white girl with red hair, wearing shorts, bikini top and a diamond stud stuck in her nose.

When Sam interrupted us with our drinks order—minus the warm camel's milk—Dad came over and crouched down beside my chair. "I meant what I said about seeing you blossom." He laid his hand on my arm and spoke quietly to me, "I know you are a free spirit and will do whatever urges you. I'm not blind, Riley—I've noticed the way you and Nagya interact. Of course I want what is best for you, but you are the one to choose your own destiny. That's all I'm going to say," he said, looking into my eyes.

"Oh, Dad! I love you so," I whispered, my lips trembling. He kissed my cheek and went back to his place at the table.

When we had finished eating, the manager introduced herself. "I am Margaret, and I am from Zanzibar. It has been a pleasure to serve you in our restaurant. Please give my blessings to East Africa when you return," she said graciously, shaking hands with us.

After she had gone, Chief Jallaba chuckled and said, "See, woman managing man! Times are changing: here in Canada, but more importantly in Africa."

"Well," I chirped, ready to throw myself into a debate, "what about some of the girls guiding customers to the dinner table just like the boys leading camels to the trough back home."

"You've certainly opened up a debatable topic, Riley," said Nagya. "How do you explain our female driver? Isn't it man's work to operate machinery?"

Gabbra came to my rescue. "What about the

guy who took our order? Didn't you say it was women's work? And the men in the kitchen washing and cooking? Shouldn't women be doing that job, Nagya?" she said, teasingly.

Chief Jallaba and my father rose quickly from their seats.

"*Bwana* Forbes and I will leave. We have many things to discuss before my return to Africa," said the Chief. "I see you three have much to talk about and, besides, there is a band from Zanzibar about to start playing."

Dad told us the driver would return in two hours. "Until then, Nagya will take good care of you girls."

Nagya threw his hands in the air in mock surrender.

"I guess that means I'll finally be doing a *real* man's job—herding women," he quipped.

As soon as her father had left the restaurant, Gabbra introduced her brother to Sam, whose shift of waiting tables had finished.

"Nagya, this is my friend Sam, the medical student I told you about. He would like to join us." Despite a strained look on Nagya's face, both men shook hands politely and sat down.

"Nagya, I want to set the record straight," said Gabbra, slanting her eyes toward Sam. "I want to honour our Borana culture, but we cannot turn back the pages of history. I have broken the promise that I gave our mother before she was...before the *Shifta* took her, and I have decided not to live the rest of my life in Dumbuluk."

Nagya remained silent, knowing this to be his destiny too.

"Help me out, Nagya. Speak to me. I feel like I'm drowning here," said Gabbra, sounding desperate. "Sam is from a new generation in Somalia. We simply have to learn how to adapt to both worlds. Later on, Sam and I want to travel with you to drought-ridden areas as 'flying doctors'. We believe we can help keep the vanishing tribes alive."

Sam spoke. "Gabbra told me something of her past. Please believe me, Nagya, when I apologise sincerely for the wrongdoings of Somali bandits. They are vermin and a disgrace to my race. With the help of Flying Doctors Unlimited, an emergency supply of food and water, and the end of this horrible drought, there will be no need for *Shifta* to steal from their neighbours in Kenya.

"Let me explain how I can see two sides of Gabbra's vision and the reason she feels she is letting her mother down."

Nobody spoke, but Sam continued anyway. "First, the negative side. With foreign aid will come the breakdown of culture and the possible demise of Boranas. Educated children will leave their villages and enter major cities, questioning both family values and traditions."

I watched Sam take a deep breath as he glanced into Nagya's hostile-looking eyes. Without flinching, he said, "Relief aid will give people food to which they are not accustomed, and irrigation of pastures would use well-water so fast, it's possible there may not be enough for future years."

With a look of amusement on his face, Nagya broke the silence. "And what of the positive side, man of Somalia? Or is it only doom you wish to inform us about?"

"I'll tell you," interrupted Gabbra, sharply. "Soon the rains will come, as predicted. Here's the positive side. Children must have an education and that includes girls. Boranas will be kept healthy with frequent visits from flying doctors…"

I'd had enough of their bickering. Had they forgotten about all my efforts to bring pipes and pumps to northern Kenya?

"Now you have to listen to *me*," I said, interrupting my friend.

"Ah! A blast of fresh air!" announced Nagya, slapping his hand down on the table.

"You know the answers already, Nagya, but I'm going to remind you about the discussions we had when you were recovering from the bandit attack," I said, ignoring his sarcasm. "People rely on camels for milk, meat, and transportation. But, if we sell most of the camels to buy seed, we can grow crops and pasture and eventually build a bigger and more stable community village, and go back to rearing goats and cows. We have a semi-desert now which will continue to erode if we continue the way we are. I think we need to irrigate and reclaim land back from the desert before it's too late."

"Good debating points," chuckled Nagya, pursing his lips and nodding like an Elder.

I beamed at him. "International consultants will show us how to operate the solar pump system that will pump water down the pipes and into the village," I said. "We'll bring in an irrigation system for pastures, once we confirm there is enough supply of underground spring water. It'll work, I promise you. Everything has to change. You have all started the change by coming to Canada for your education."

"I didn't have a choice," Gabbra said, quietly. "Father sent me away. But I do not regret it." She glanced quickly at Sam. I recalled Chief Jallaba saying he wanted his daughter to be educated, and did not want her to suffer the female circumcision tradition of their people.

"Gabbra will encourage the older men and women to keep the traditional stories and songs and culture alive," Sam suggested. "The old men can melt down aluminum cooking pots, and the girls will make and sell one-of-a-kind beaded necklaces to pay for livestock and seeds. It's a success story."

"Oh, I see, Sam," said Nagya, with a scornful tone to his voice. "Now we're bringing in a truckload of metal kitchenware so we can sell jewellery to tourists."

Sam merely smiled at him.

"I presume we have all come to a meeting of the minds," continued Nagya. "We're agreeing that cultural change is inevitable. However, it's up to my father and I to talk the Elders into either changing or becoming *the lost tribe*. It will be a slow transformation, but the Elders have the power to persuade both men and women to work together."

Nagya turned to Gabbra. "My sister, I know you're struggling with the oath you took, but I believe you've come to terms with it."

Both men excused themselves and walked outside into the fresh night air.

After a moment, I reached over and grabbed Gabbra's arm gently. "Do you think that Nagya really likes me, even though Ayasha…"

She interrupted me. "Of course he does. Nagya simply adores you," she said. "My little friend, I admire you for all your amazing efforts in trying to bring water to my village."

I looked down at the black and white tiled floor.

"Riley," she said, quietly, pulling her chair closer to me, "I am not destined to marry a Borana tribesman—I've spent too long away from home," she confessed. "I've told you before, I cannot return to a lonely life as the wife of a nomad. I don't want to live in a *manyatta,* have several kids and do boring chores, or obedient to a husband and follow the rules made by Elders."

"And you really love Sam, don't you?" I whispered. "Is Nagya angry with you because he is from a different tribe? Will I ever see you again when you travel with Sam?"

"Always these questions! My heart is with Sam, I believe he's my soul mate. I yearn to be with him and help the sick in Africa after I graduate from medical school. We will have a great future together," she said, dreamily. "But even if you and I go our separate ways after we graduate, I'll never forget you, my friend. I'll always wear your butterfly necklace." She hugged me as though she did not want to let go.

Then she looked at me strangely. "Perhaps it's because I'm feeling a bit guilty for loving Sam, but recently I've been hearing strange whispers in the night, warning me about breaking the oath I made to my mother—of keeping the culture alive and leading by example."

I felt I was scrabbling for words in a cauldron of alphabet soup.

"Have you ever had to wrestle with a

powerful force that controls your destiny?" she asked. It was rare for Gabbra to talk in such a mysterious manner. The last time she sounded desperate was back at the *manyatta* when Nagya was wounded by *Shifta* bandits, and she realized her brother might die without proper medicine.

I hesitated. "I'm not sure where you're going with this, Gabbra, but although I'm impulsive at times, I try to follow my Christian faith. I'm an optimist. My destiny is guided by positive thoughts and actions—with a little bit of luck thrown in by an Irish pixy." I thought she would laugh with me, but she didn't.

"Riley, I'm feeling nauseous and scared," she said, her hands shaking noticeably. "I have bad vibes about going back to Dumbuluk this summer. It's almost as if…"

She put her hand up to her mouth and, without another word, bolted for the washroom.

Aluminum necklaces of the Borana tribe.

Chapter 12

WARRIOR IN THE CITY

IN THE DIM LIGHT of the Zanzibar Club, a lone guitar player crooned *Malaika,* which Nagya told me meant *My Angel.* A large hand nestled on top of my own, like a warm glove.

"Would you like to dance?" Nagya's eyes flashed an invitation.

Dancing brought back sharp memories of the Borana girls and warriors celebrating after the circumcision ceremony. Flickering fire, flirtation, bodies glistening with sweat, hypnotic rhythm of drums and exotic dancing plagued my mind. Was he thinking of Ayasha when he heard that familiar African drumming?

"I think I'll wait for the fast song," I stammered. My feelings were muddled, uncertain, confused, like reaching into a bag of assorted jelly beans and finding a liquorice snake.

Suddenly, every African instrument imaginable was brought to life—a crazy mixture of Afro-American music that made the toes tap and brought a smile to the lips. How appropriate, I thought, as a Zanzibari singer belted out the old familiar song *Hakuna Matata—There is no problem.*

"Okay, what about *this* one!" shouted Nagya, grabbing me by the arm and hauling me to my feet. I forgot about the dancers of Dumbuluk because I became one of them as Nagya and I danced in tribal fashion. We flung our arms high above our heads and jumped as though our feet were attached to rubber springs. He held firmly around the waist, raising me in the air, swirling round and round as the musicians took us to feverish heights. I was so happy I didn't want the night to end.

"I feel like I'm at home in Dumbuluk," shouted Nagya. "I'm looking at my beautiful little Borana girl leaping so sweetly in front of me."

Our driver Mae-Lee waved at us from the entrance to indicate it was time to leave. I watched as Sam held Gabbra's hands and looked tenderly into her eyes for a very long time before we left the club.

"Please drive along the seawall through Stanley Park before we head home," I said to Mae-Lee.

Nagya sat up front, while Gabbra and I sat in the back and reminisced about our years together. As we approached the park, I noticed Nagya leaning forward in his seat, as though he was trying to focus on something in the distance.

"Mae-Lee, stop the car," he commanded urgently. "Let me out right here. Drive the girls further down the block and wait for me."

Gabbra and I stared at one another.

"What are you doing, brother?" asked Gabbra. She put her hand gently on his shoulder, but he shrugged it off.

"Nagya, what's happening?" I said, beginning to panic. "Where are you going?"

The street light shone through the rear window. When he turned round to face us, his eyes held a strange, steel-grey hardness that frightened me.

"A girl is being attacked by two men. Look over there," he said, pointing to the dimly-lit entrance of the park.

"Nagya, this has nothing to do with you. It's none of your business," I shouted at him, leaning over and tugging his arm.

"It has *everything* to do with me. Isn't this your *manyatta*, Riley? Isn't this part of you? Don't you care what happens to that girl?"

"It's *not* a *manyatta*!" I yelled, gripping his shoulder. "You're *not* in Africa, and you don't have to act like Superman *here*!"

"What's the difference, Riley? Vancouver or Dumbuluk? There are thugs all over the world. My mother was attacked. It could happen to my sister—or even you. Now let me go!"

Nagya struggled and shot out of the car. We watched him bolt back to the park, edging close to the high, manicured hedge and disappear.

"You can't stop him, Riley," said Gabbra, softly. "He's been educated in a white-man's world, but he can't sit back and watch some innocent person being bullied. It's his warrior training. They're *Shifta* bandits to him."

Mae-Lee drove to the end of the block and turned off the lights. While she was calling the police on her cell phone, I looked back and saw two scruffy-looking men re-emerge in the dim light, dragging their screaming victim. One of the men had a knife aimed at the girl's throat; the other grabbed her purse.

"Look! Nagya has climbed a tree right above them, and he's found a long stick," said Mae-Lee. Nagya must have snapped off a branch to use as a spear—a weapon he was familiar with in times of danger.

We watched as Nagya pounced, surprising them with an air-ambush. The girl was released as soon as he landed on the thug holding her. Nagya prodded him into the bushes with his spear before turning to attack the second guy who had grabbed the girl by the hair.

The thief in the bushes recovered himself and slashed Nagya's arm with a knife. Nagya swirled round and stabbed him in the leg with the end of the branch. Nagya, bleeding from his knife-wound, shouted something to the girl. She twisted herself free and ran to Nagya, while her assailant reached inside his jacket and pulled out an object that was black and shiny.

"Gabbra, he's got a gun!" I screamed.

Feeling utterly helpless, I watched Nagya grasp the girl's hand and push her behind him for protection. Shoving the thug with the gun to the ground, he spun his spear around to a horizontal position and pinned the bandit's arms down so tightly that it looked like he couldn't move.

It all happened so quickly. All three of us in the car gasped when the weapon exploded during the confusion. Did he shoot the girl? Did he shoot Nagya?

"There's blood oozing from Nagya's thigh! Oh my God, Gabbra, Nagya's been shot!" I shrieked, as Nagya sprawled on top of the thief who was trying to wriggle free. Nagya punched him swiftly in the head, snatched the gun out of the man's hand and sent it spinning down the sidewalk. The girl helped Nagya to his feet. She stooped to pick up her purse and ran barefoot from the park, her long black hair swinging from side to side, before she disappeared around the corner.

Mae-Lee backed up the car as Nagya limped slowly toward us. Lights flashed and sirens whined as the police cruiser pulled up behind us. I ran to Nagya. With his good arm around my shoulders, I helped him walk to our car, while the muggers were hauled into the van.

"Thank you, sir," said one policeman, after taking a statement from Nagya. "Too much thuggery on the streets these days, eh? That young girl was lucky, but others are not so fortunate. You're bleeding. Are you okay?"

"Just a little scratch," said Nagya. "Goodnight, sir," and he slumped into the back seat beside Gabbra.

Blood seeped through a hole in Nagya's black pants; his shirt sleeve was slashed and also stained a brilliant red.

"Not so bad," sighed Nagya. "Just a little war wound. That was man's work, Riley. It's a *guy* thing." Then he drifted into unconsciousness.

"I'm taking Mr. Nagya immediately to the hospital," said Mae-Lee, turning to look at

Gabbra.

Gabbra nodded. "Riley, hold Nagya's head in your arms and cover him with your coat to keep him warm. Raise his arm to reduce blood from the wound. I'll wrap my shawl tightly round the cut so that pressure is maintained. I'll put into practise what I've been reading in the library," she was saying. "I'll hold his upper thigh and press hard with both hands to stop the bleeding." I'll never forget her efficiency, capability and medical knowledge, and I knew she would be a very good doctor one day.

"Drive a bit faster, Mae-Lee. He's bleeding badly," said Gabbra.

Shivering and frightened, I looked up at Gabbra for reassurance. Gabbra was calm in situations like this. After all, it wasn't so long ago that she had tended to the wounded warriors in Dumbuluk after the *Shifta* attack.

I thought back to when Nagya rescued me from the bottom of the well. Concerned and anxious, he had taken care of me. Now it was I who cradled Nagya in my arms, to keep him warm.

As soon as we arrived at St. Paul's Hospital, Nagya was whisked away on a stretcher. In the waiting room, Gabbra stared into space, Mae-Lee flipped through a magazine, and I paced up and down the corridors. I looked at my watch. Midnight on the dot. It seemed like an eternity until the surgeon walked toward me, removing his mask.

"You must be Riley and Gabbra," he said, cheerfully. "We have removed the bullet successfully, and now you'll want to visit Nagya. I'll warn you, he's very groggy from the anaesthetic."

Nagya grinned sleepily at us as we stood in a row, looking down at him. He reached out to catch my hand.

"This time I'm in a clean hospital with nurses in uniform," he said, slurring his words. "And when I woke up I thought it was Gabbra tending to my wounds back in Dumbuluk."

Gabbra smiled at him.

"But when I focused properly," Nagya continued, "I saw that my nurse was a black Nigerian male."

I don't think he heard our laughter because his eyes closed and he sank back sleepily into his pillow.

Chapter 13

CURSE OF THE BROKEN OATH

NAGYA RECOVERED QUICKLY, and returned to flight school. He spent several more weeks in training, and was going to get his commercial pilot's licence. He told us that he would drive down to see us at school as soon as he had received his certificates.

That unexpected visit came during a lunch break while we were sitting on the steps outside the library. Gabbra was poking around in her bowl of rice—picking it out one grain at a time, while I made rustling sounds with the local newspaper, searching for my horoscope.

"A new cycle of growth and adventure begins this month. Success is inevitable. Beware suspicious behaviour from colleagues during the full moon..." I read out loud, but Gabbra was not listening.

She stood up quickly, spilling her bowl of rice and exclaimed, "Nagya, you're here! You've graduated! Now you can fly us anywhere in the world."

I looked up from my newspaper, and there was Nagya, walking up the steps toward us.

Gabbra's out-of-character outburst caught the attention of other students. Not only did Nagya entertain Gabbra and me, but an audience of female admirers drew closer, eager to hear him speak. Like me, he loved to inspire his listeners.

"You know what they do to you after you graduate from this bush pilot school?" he said, eyeing his assembly of women. Without waiting for an answer, he continued. "The guys rip the back off your shirt and staple it to the wall of the hangar where they keep the planes."

"Now you're talking!" said one of the girls.

"I learned from the best instructor," said Nagya, obviously enjoying himself. "He's a cussing, grumpy old Canadian bush pilot who used to operate a sea plane over rugged coastlines. He's known as the Old Coast Dog, and he said you only get that name by flying in extremely scary conditions in the Arctic Circle." The girls edged nearer, fascinated.

Encouraged by this show of flirtatious behaviour, he kept us spellbound with his stories. When the bell rang, the giggling girls returned reluctantly to class, looking over their shoulders as they smiled and waved at him.

Gabbra and I shook our heads. "Those girls are so brazen," she said, as we walked Nagya over to his car.

"I will be going back to Dumbuluk tomorrow," he announced, suddenly.

"Why now?" I demanded. "Can't you wait till we all go for summer vacation? Come on, Nagya! It's only two weeks away."

"I wish I could join you, Nagya" said Gabbra. "You're going to need my help."

"It's an emergency United Nations humanitarian operation," he explained. "Now that I'm a qualified pilot, my father called from Nairobi, asking me to come as soon as possible to help fly supplies into areas north of Dumbuluk. It's a huge undertaking, and the first load has gone already."

When Nagya left, I saw a crowd of girls talking to Gabbra in the school corridor.

"Who is that dark, gorgeous-looking stranger, Gabbra?" one of them asked.

She just smiled, grabbed my arm and we

walked back to class.

It seemed an eternity before the start of our summer vacation but finally Dad, Gabbra and I flew the many hours, via Nairobi, to Dumbuluk. Gabbra's father met us at the airstrip with the LandRover. My father had to fly back immediately to Nairobi. His company was sending him on another emergency assignment for several weeks.

"I'll radio-call Nagya when I'm ready to fly back in," he said to the Chief. "It would probably save time if you brought the girls here to the airstrip." He was talking about the end of our long holiday in Dumbuluk when he would fly us back to Nairobi, then home to Vancouver.

Dad leaned out of the cockpit window and blew me a kiss. "Gabbra," said Dad, laughing, "I hope you and Nagya will keep an eye on my daughter!"

I smiled to myself. This time I did not mind being left behind with Nagya and Gabbra. Dad's small Cessna roared down the bumpy track and we watched till it was a tiny speck in the sky.

"I am so glad to see you both," said Chief Jallaba, hugging his daughter and shaking me by the hand. "You'll be anxious to see the pipes and solar equipment that have just been delivered to the well. Nagya should be back soon to help with the pipeline."

Our trip back to the *manyatta* took longer this time because we made a detour to the well where three African workmen were busy unloading a solar-powered water pump from one of the trucks.

"*Jambo,* hello, Miss Riley," said one of the workers. "Please let me show you around. My name is Mathenge, and this is Kamau and Kimathi. We are from the Kikuyu tribe. We drove up here from Nairobi and started working on the pipeline last week. After we've assembled the pipeline, the idea is to dig down fifty feet." Gabbra shaded her eyes with her hands as Mathenge pointed to the pipeline that began to snake its way in the direction of the *manyatta*.

"Next to the well are twenty-four solar panels sitting, right now, on top of a giant box," Mathenge said.

"Thank you, Mathenge," I smiled at him. "I'm curious to see the system in operation. How does it actually work?" I asked.

"The solar panels will be mounted on a fixed structure," Mathenge answered. "The panels provide power to pump fresh water out of the well at ten gallons per minute. Later we'll be looking into irrigating the pastures."

"Let me say something," said the man called Kamau. "A continuous supply of fresh spring water will move through the line into a huge fifteen-hundred-gallon storage tank in the new

Borana community village that will be built closer to the well."

"But what about at night when there is no sun?" asked Gabbra.

"The solar panels generate power when the sun is out and the pumps use the stored power when the sun is down," explained Mathenge.

We drank refreshingly sweet, milky tea with the crew, who sat on their haunches around what Mathenge called a *jiko,* a small portable metal stove with hot coals in the bottom part.

"What are you cooking, Kamau?" I asked, looking skeptically at a thick white mass bubbling and heaving in a pot on top of the stove.

"It's called *posho*—ground maize-meal and water—and it fills our bellies," said Kamau with a deep laugh.

Chief Jallaba told us that he had called a meeting of the village. "Nagya joined me to introduce the idea of change and try to persuade our people to sell a third of their animals for cash to buy seed and pasture for livestock," explained the Chief. "The Elders are having yet another private discussion about the future of Dumbuluk, but they understand it may be wise to build a pipeline."

"How will they maintain the solar pump?" asked Gabbra.

Kamau explained, "Every six weeks, an expert from Nairobi will come and inspect the system."

"And irrigation?" I said.

"Water from the pipes will irrigate the crops, but this will be done after the tank has been installed," said the Chief. "I agree with Nagya that building a village and growing crops will be a more secure life; we won't have to keep looking for new pastures. This may be our only chance of saving our people if this drought cycle continues to get worse," he said.

"We could still have a herd of camels and perhaps some cows, goats and fat-tailed sheep," suggested Gabbra. "I'm surprised that the Elders agreed to all this change and interference, Father. This is a dramatic cultural shift. Will they be able to adapt? Our people are used to travelling with their camels to fetch water. They don't know how to grow crops, and they are unaccustomed to residing in one place. And what about Ayasha? I'm worried…"

"I didn't say they *agreed*, or that they are totally convinced," interrupted her father, shaking his head gravely. "The idea of a village with stores, medical dispensary and possibly even a school was met with great skepticism, but I am trying to reassure our people that change is inevitable for Boranas, especially at a time like this when whole clans can be wiped out by drought."

I looked up sharply at the Chief, who was still talking. "Although the Elders usually respect my suggestions, I admit they are bewildered right now, but I know my people will be satisfied when they see water flowing from pipes into a reservoir at a new village," he said. "Now let's go home."

As we climbed into the LandRover, I nudged Gabbra gently. "You sounded a bit negative about the Elders agreeing to change."

"I have to question my father's thought process. He expects it of me," she said. "I'll speak to the Elders myself, though. First I want to expand on the changes my father has discussed with them. I think they need some reassurance that it can—and must—work with outside help. You see, Riley, from experience I know they take a long time to reach a decision, but it is always the right one. Then I'll have to convince them about my future plans—and they won't be pleased at first…"

I interrupted her. "Why did you mention Ayasha? Why are you so worried about her?"

Gabbra was quiet for a moment. "Ayasha's a bright girl, Riley, but she might not be able to cope with all the extreme changes being made. She needs help…"

"Why do you say that?" I snapped. "Can't she talk to the Elders and find out what's being planned?"

"No, because she cannot speak."

"What?" I was stunned, as though shock waves were electrocuting my brain.

"Ayasha's been unable to talk since she was eight years old," said Gabbra. "She understands exactly what's going on and she can hear me. I know what she's trying to say by her hand movement and eye contact."

Like Ayasha, I, too, was unable to speak. I began to regret the resentment that had been growing like venom inside me, and wondered how she would ever be able to express her feelings like an ordinary person.

Although Nagya indicated he enjoyed my company the night he and I had danced at the Zanzibar Club, I could not erase the memory of Ayasha and Nagya together at the warriors' ceremonial dance, smiling happily, wiggling their glistening bodies together, touching. Most of all, the way he looked at her.

Not one word was spoken all the way back to the *manyatta*, for we were each in our own silent world with only thoughts for company.

I dropped both backpacks onto the camel skin bedding in our old hut while we changed into traditional clothes. The cowrie shells stitched on the bottom of Gabbra's leather skirt made a clicking sound as she moved around.

"Gabbra," I said, "I've been thinking about what you said in the LandRover and I have a question. It involves Ayasha and…"

"Not now, Riley," she interrupted. "It's a painful topic to me and I don't want to discuss it at the moment. As you can see, I'm a bit preoccupied. I'm going right now to talk to the Elders because I can see they're sitting with Kallu the Head Elder under the Meeting Tree. That's where they settle any questions and problems that arise. I promise I will tell you about Ayasha later."

More than ever I wanted desperately to see Nagya. I needed his warm reassurance to flow into my own reservoir of unanswered questions.

Nagya took a break from the humanitarian aid project in northern Kenya and returned to Dumbuluk to help the crew dig a trench for the water pipeline that was advancing, albeit slowly, toward the proposed new village.

The workmen arrived by LandRover to pick him up at the *manyatta*. "Remember the little hill leading away from the thorn enclosure to the well?" he said. "That's where we'll set up camp to eat and sleep. I'll get up with those guys as soon as it's light, and work till the sun goes down."

He was so preoccupied with the plans that I could not talk to him privately. Ten minutes later, he leapt into the LandRover with Mathenge, Kamau and Kimathi, leaving a blanket of dust behind them.

Early one morning I decided to ride out by camel and see how they had progressed, admitting to myself that I really needed to be with Nagya.

I think my camel, Clarence, became accustomed to me handling him, remembering our episode down at the well and, with water and food strapped to his side, he plodded along at a brisk pace down the familiar track. While I swayed from side to side, I had the irresistible urge to sing. Gabbra would have winced if she had heard me bellowing her special song with such raucousness, but Clarence didn't seem to mind. Anyway, my loud singing kept us both calm and unruffled.

It did not seem long before we were in range of the water well area. Holding my hand up to shade my eyes from the sun, I could see a truck packed high with pipes, and four figures dragging one of the long metal pipes out of the back.

"Nagya!" I shouted, as we got closer, "I'm going to the well first. I'll be right back. Clarence needs water." He waved to me in recognition and carried on working.

Surveying the quiet barren land around me, I was impressed at the distance Nagya and his crew had covered with the pipeline in only a few days. I found a huge pile of neatly stacked pipes under an Acacia tree on the brow of the hill where the camp was set up and, recognizing the thorn enclosure that surrounded the well, I led Clarence down to the trough. Nagya must have fetched water from the bottom of the well because the trough was filled.

Close by, the solar panel system was half assembled. As I sat on the lip of the well, I was conscious of how my life had changed in only a few months. A feeling of pride enveloped me, and I knew all the work I'd done to help raise money for the pipeline project meant the future and survival of Nagya's people, although I wondered what the Elders thought of my contribution to their lives.

After Clarence slurped and snorted as much water as he could take, I guided him, still dripping water, up to the camp. Nagya and the crew had returned with the truck and were loading up more pipes from the stack for the next day's work.

As I tethered my camel, the Africans dropped what they were doing and ran in all directions from the truck, screaming "Nyoka! Nyoka!"

Nagya headed toward me, shouting and waving his arms in the air. "Keep back, Riley. There's a venomous carpet viper inside one of the pipes. It will strike very quickly."

Alarmed, I watched as he broke off a branch from the Acacia tree. With a sharp knife, he split the end, and pinched the snake's neck firmly between the two prongs.

"Why is it making that noise, Nagya?"

"The viper rasps its very rough scales together to scare off intruders," he replied, concentrating on getting a better grip. "It's a nocturnal reptile. See its big eyes?" Nagya flicked the one-foot viper into the air. It crash-landed into a bush and slithered to the ground. I could see its *S*-shaped tracks in the sand as it meandered quickly away from us.

"It's very odd for it to get into a smooth pipe," said Nagya, looking mystified. "Vipers do not climb."

Nagya set up another little tent for me because it was too late to travel back to the *manyatta*. Kamau parked the truck close to the camp while Mathenge gathered sticks for a fire. Kimathi looked up when he saw me standing beside him.

"I'm making *posho*," he said, grinning widely. "Eat supper with us, Miss Riley," he said invitingly, while he stirred the thick white porridge mixture inside a black pot.

That evening, we scooped *posho* out of the pot with our fingers, while the three Kikuyu men entertained us with wonderful stories about their own cultural traditions and beliefs.

Nagya said he wanted to discuss the day's progress with the others before he went to bed and, as I stood up to leave, he reached out and caught my hand.

"Good night, Riley-girl. I'll ride back with you to the *manyatta* in the morning."

Kamau called out to me, "In Swahili, we say *Lala salaama kijana,* which means *Sleep well little one.*"

Raising the flaps of my small tent, I felt like a contented bird coming home to roost. I crouched low, shuffling to get inside my little nest of musty-smelling camel skins—uncomfortable but warm. Hyenas laughed with such fits of ridiculous giggling that I could not sleep. Perhaps the full moon was sending them crazy. I was also deafened by the high-pitched hissing of invisible crickets.

Despite the snuffles and snores of the four men in their big tent, I slept well. But some time during the silent early hours of the morning, something woke me up. The crickets had stopped singing and the hyenas had quitted their crazy chuckling, but it wasn't only the hoot of an owl that disturbed my dreams. I heard the familiar clicking sound of a leather skirt decorated with cowrie shells, and the soft thud of bare feet padding off into the distance.

"Gabbra, is that you?" I murmured. Of course Gabbra was not there—she was back at the *manyatta,* I told myself. Now fully awake, I sat up and looked around. I thought I heard the faint sound of tinkling glass, like wind chimes in the distance, and hooves hammering softly along the sand. I dismissed my disturbed thoughts and snuggled back under the hairy camel skin.

Hours later, I awoke again to the sound of footsteps outside my tent and someone unzipping the flap. A flood of light hit me in the face, forcing me to sit up and open my eyes. Nagya crouched at the entrance.

"Riley, get up. Somebody has sabotaged our solar panels," he said, angrily.

"Who? Why do you say sabotaged?" I asked.

"I don't know who did it, but the whole thing has been deliberately smashed. Mathenge and Kamau went down to the well early this morning to fill up their *gourds*, and they found the equipment destroyed. They woke me up to tell me. When you're ready, we'll go and see what we can salvage."

Had I been dreaming, or did I really hear someone tampering with the equipment last night? I told Nagya about the tinkling sounds, the click of leather skirts and thud of hooves. He stared at me but said nothing.

The workers drove back to where the pipeline was in progress. Nagya fetched Clarence and, pulling me up behind him, we headed down to the well. As the early morning sun blazed on my back, Nagya showed me the damaged solar equipment. It looked like a huge rock had been dropped on the apparatus and then beaten with a crowbar.

Disappointed, sad and dejected, I mumbled to Nagya, "It's a hopeless situation. We're doomed. Something or somebody is stopping us from bringing water to the village…"

I was interrupted by fearful roars of anger further down the pipeline. I whirled round to see where the cries were coming from. "What's going on, Nagya?"

"Sounds like more trouble," he said. "I'd better go and see."

"Don't leave me. I'm coming with you," I said, grabbing his arm.

We found the three men from Nairobi sitting on their haunches, drinking tea. They sat in silence and refused to work. When Nagya talked to them, I saw them pointing to the last silver pipe they had assembled the day before.

"*Kinyonga. Shitani.* A chameleon. A devil spirit is on the pipe. We cannot stay here. We will not work any more," said Mathenge, without looking up from his cup of tea.

"Come and see," said Nagya, beckoning to me.

I stared, fascinated, at a scaly-skinned five-inch chameleon ambling painstakingly slowly along the end pipe. One arm was poised in the air which it placed carefully down, followed by the next arm. Devilish bulbous eyes swivelled around from back to front, each eye moving independently, and its lengthy tail was curled up tightly like the end of a mottled green fern found deep in the forest. With lightning speed, its elongated sticky tongue—which was as long as its body—darted out and caught a black bug.

"Flap-necked chameleon," observed Nagya. "Probably a male because of its size. It's trying to change colour right now on the silver-grey pipe."

"You mean if it was walking on something red it might explode?" I smirked.

Nagya grinned at me. "Actually, it's not a funny situation. A lot of tribes hate chameleons. Although the creature is harmless, these guys are literally terrified of them. They think the chameleon is venomous and will bring bad luck. These guys won't work till the offending creature has been taken away," he explained.

Nagya lifted the chameleon carefully off the pipe and released it into the bushes far away.

"Tell me why you hate chameleons," I asked the African workers.

Kimathi, put down his cup and looked suspiciously from side to side. "The Kikuyu tribe dislikes it intensely. The story that's handed down for generations goes like this. God, or *Ngai*, sent a cheetah, an elephant and a chameleon out to an all-black world to bring the people to a central water hole to bathe so that they would become white."

Then Mathenge stood up. "I'll tell the story now. The cheetah was very swift, so when he got to Europe, all the people who bathed in the pool became white. The elephant plodded across to South East Asia, but the water was becoming rather muddy, and people turned a brown colour."

Kimathi's eyes widened. "Now there was hardly any water left in the pool because the chameleon was too slow to reach Africa," he said. "So there was only enough water to turn the soles of their feet and the palms of their hands white, and that is why there are so many black people in the world."

Mathenge looked around at his audience, his eyes so big they appeared to be stuck. "We are proud to be black, but Tanzanians tell us that later on, *Ngai* sent another chameleon messenger to save the world from death. The chameleon was so cautious and hesitant that he arrived too late to warn everyone and all the mortals died. That is why we call him the devil because we fear and hate him at the same time," said Mathenge.

Only when Nagya reassured them that the chameleon had gone did the crew return to laying the pipeline, taking care not to touch the area where the 'devil' had been.

Nagya took me aside. "I think someone is sabotaging any effort to bring change to Dumbuluk. Someone planted that chameleon in a third attempt to frighten the workers off."

I had a gnawing ache of disappointment in the pit of my stomach. I wrestled with angry questions of why anyone would destroy all our efforts to bring life-saving progress to this part of the world.

Nagya and I left the Kikuyu workers at the

well and rode the camel back to the *manyatta,* silent with our own thoughts.

The sun was high above us when we arrived. Nagya led Clarence to his tethering post with the other camels. I felt weary from our trip, and looked forward to sharing a cup of sweet, milky tea with Gabbra. I had so much to tell her, especially of the strange ruckus going on back at the well.

I hoped Gabbra would be waiting for me outside our hut, but only my little friend Jillo was there to welcome me, and he looked agitated. He jumped up and down when he saw me and pulled my arm, talking fast in a high-pitched voice. Pointing at the Head Elder's hut, he shouted loudly, trying to make me understand.

"Jillo, it's Kallu's hut. So what?"

Undaunted, he grabbed my hand and ran with me to Nagya's sleeping quarters, where he waited respectfully until Nagya was ready to hear him.

"Nagya," I said, "the boy is trying to tell me something."

Nagya listened intently as Jillo talked excitedly, again using his arms to point in the direction of the Elders' quarters, then Ayasha's hut, and finally the camel's route toward the well.

Nagya jumped to his feet and ran swiftly to

where the camels were tethered. Before I could stop him, he headed his own camel in the direction of the well, beating the animal with his stick and kicking it in the ribs to make it go faster. All I could hear was the soft thud of camel feet pounding down the rough, winding track, startling several mourning doves who flapped, frightened, into the swirling dust.

Jillo sat beside me in the cool shade of the hut while Nagya was gone. He did not smile, but perched quietly, studying the pictures in his book of *Jack and the Beanstalk*. I was concerned about his odd behaviour. Every now and then he looked up at me, and when I put an arm around him, he snuggled closer, as though he wanted comfort from whatever was worrying him. Finally, he ran off to join his friends.

Sitting on a warm rock, I used the last rays of the evening sun to scribble in my journal. When I heard the familiar soft pad of a camel returning home, I slammed my note-book shut and started to walk over to meet Nagya.

As the camel entered the *manyatta*, Nagya shouted in a strangled voice I did not recognise. I stood very still, not believing what I was seeing or hearing. My skin prickled, and I felt for a heartbeat that didn't seem to want to thump.

He cradled a body wrapped up in his *shuka*, while Ayasha, running beside the slobbering camel, held on to a bare leg dangling limp and lifeless.

Ayasha howled like a wounded animal. Although I was astounded at hearing her voice for the first time, I shivered with fright. It was the most fearful sound I had ever heard—neither animal nor human. I felt my legs go weak and trembly as I fought my way in slow motion through a maze of wailing and ululating women. When the camels bawled in alarm, I knew something terrible had happened. My mouth went dry. I remember that same feeling of panic when I heard Dad cry the day my mother left us.

Listening to Ayasha's deafening laments, I suspected Fate would again affect my destiny.

A Borana girl very
much like Ayasha.

Chapter 14

THE GIRL WITHOUT A FACE

GABBRA WAS IN A COMA, barely alive. I think Nagya knew what he might discover after his urgent discussion with Jillo.

Nagya found me sitting, motionless and shocked, on a heap of soft sand outside my hut. Hot tears poured down my face like a flash-flood flowing down a dry river bed.

"I found her unconscious beside the well," said Nagya, stone-faced, like the land around him.

A dull cement-grey glazed across his usually black sparkling eyes.

"I unclasped the necklace from around Gabbra's neck because it was restricting her," he said, hoarsely. "Here, take care of it."

The gold butterfly pendant I had given Gabbra for her sixteenth birthday lay in the palm of my hand. My eyes misted as I tried to concentrate on the tiny inscription I'd had engraved at the back, *"Friends Forever—Gabbra and Riley."*

Nagya slumped down on his knees near the entrance of his father's hut and closed his eyes, murmuring to himself. I followed Chief Jallaba inside as he and two of the women carried Gabbra and laid her on a bed of camel skins. With her hair smoothed out around her and eyes closed, Gabbra looked like she was sleeping. Suddenly, her body went into quick spasms.

"Why is she twitching like that?" I whispered to the Chief.

Gabbra's father did not look up to answer me. "Snake venom."

I stared at him for a few seconds. With a rude slap of reality, I knew she had probably been poisoned. Gabbra herself had pointed out the deadly poisonous spitting cobra draped around a tall termite hill when we were travelling with the Chief during spring break. She had told me that when the snake's crystallized neurotoxin was mixed with camel milk, the victim couldn't tell anything was wrong and usually died soon after swallowing the mixture.

"Someone has tried to murder her," said the Chief. "Tell Nagya to protect Ayasha."

My mind was confused. What was the connection between Ayasha and Gabbra? I understood why Ayasha was so upset with Gabbra's alarming condition, but what caused her to speak—or howl—for the first time in years? And why did the Chief want Nagya to protect her?

I heard scuffling outside. The women ran out of the hut, screaming and wailing as the Chief and I witnessed an astonishing display.

Nagya stood swaying in a trance-like state at the entrance of the hut, seeming to stare unblinking at something in the distance. His face glistened with sweat, the whites of his eyes rolled up and he fell on his back, writhing and beating the ground with his fists. He tried to bite his tongue while uttering groaning noises from his throat.

I attempted to help him, but the Chief held me back.

"Let him be. He has to go through the motions of anguish. His sister is in a coma and I may have lost my only daughter," he said, his chin wobbling. He paused, patted my head, and spent the night observing Gabbra.

A young girl my age guided me gently by the hand into the hut she shared with two others. I lay between them on a camel skin, but could not sleep. Like a huge rock caught in my throat, the impact of possibly losing Gabbra weighed heavily on me.

The following morning, at dawn, I joined other members of Gabbra's family outside the *manyatta* in a sad ceremony of prayer for Gabbra's dubious recovery. I watched in stunned silence as her nomadic family joined hands in the air and swayed gently from side to side, moaning softly. Nagya apparently regained his strength after a long sleep because he, too, stood with his people, praying for his sister.

The trunk of an Acacia tree murmured and creaked. I heard dry leaves rustling, and a soft wind seemed to whisper the song of our childhood hop-scotch game:

"Gabbra, Gabbra,
Abbra-Cadabbra!
If she lands on Red -
She'll fall down dead!"

I shivered at the insinuation of some of those old-fashioned witchcraft verses. But Gabbra was not going to die, was she?

Ayasha, now hysterical, could not be consoled by the women. I approached Nagya, but he ignored me and, walking swiftly to Ayasha's side, scooped her up. She put her bare arms around Nagya's neck while he sang softly to her. Staring, too numb to react, I saw Nagya cradling her in the same way he had held me once before, as he headed back toward the *manyatta*.

Emotions tangled inside me. My mind was fraught with jealousy over the relationship of Ayasha-the-snake and Nagya. I was alone: no Gabbra, no Nagya, no cuddles.

Nagya drove immediately to Nairobi to find a doctor to bring back to Gabbra.

I knelt beside her, my shoulders shaking with unabashed grief. My eyes began to leak and tears slithered down my cheeks. Gabbra lay on a bed of camel skins, her breathing so shallow that I could barely see her chest rising and falling. Five women—not wishing to leave her alone—sat together at the back of the hut, waiting silently for any movement from my friend.

I must have been dozing on and off throughout the day and into the night when a small, clammy hand slipped into mine. It was Jillo yet again. I managed a smile, and patted his head affectionately while he sat beside me.

I recalled the first time I met Jillo, when he and his giggling friends mimicked me and made me laugh. And when he wanted to show me how to trick the termites into emerging from their holes by beating the ground with sticks that sounded like rain. I remembered their laughter when they ran around pretending to be planes, and his attempt to protect me down the safety tunnel when the bandits attacked. I also thought about our trip together to get medical supplies, and his excitement when I piloted the plane.

I reached around the back of my neck and pulled off the precious aluminum beaded necklace that Gabbra had given me, curling it tenderly into a circle on the floor beside her. I could hardly breathe as I looked back on all the wonderful years we had spent together: her comforting song when I was upset, emotions that caught me by surprise when I heard her singing down the well, her calming effect on the injured warriors, and soothing women and children down the safety hole.

I remembered the camera technician's haunting explanation of Gabbra's white and ghostly shadow on my photos where her face should have been. Maybe she had an incomprehensible sixth sense about her possible looming day of judgment. After all, did she not warn me of her bad vibes about coming home again?

"Gabbra," I wailed to her. "Please give me a sign to let me know everything's going to be all right."

I wondered, for a fleeting moment, if Gabbra had heard me, for I was distracted from my lamenting by the warmth of large hands on my shoulders.

"I have come to look after the girl I love," said a familiar voice.

"Nagya, you're back!" I jumped up quickly, reaching for his hands

It was not Nagya.

Trying not to show disappointment, I looked up into Somali Sam's red-rimmed eyes.

"Hello, Riley. I flew to Nairobi as soon as possible when I heard the terrible news. Nagya picked me up and brought me here. Apparently all the Flying Doctors had left on emergencies. He's gone to his hut to get some sleep."

Sam knelt down beside me and wept into his hands. With trembling fingers, he pulled off a ring from his left hand and placed it in the middle of my necklace and the butterfly pendant. It was the gold ring engraved with a lion's head that Gabbra had given to him. Our treasures were offerings to our African Snow White who was waiting for someone to awaken her.

Sam had brought a large black medical box with him. Fascinated, I watched as he filled a rubber bag with water that was attached to a soft but flexible metal pipe. He inserted the pipe gently into Gabbra's mouth so she could take in very small amounts of water slowly—just enough to absorb fluid without choking—for the duration of her coma.

He guided me outside the hut. "We had so many plans for the future. My life will be nothing if she does not come out of this coma," he said huskily. "But she would have wanted me to work as a flying doctor here. That is her legacy…" He paused and stared at me, as though transfixed.

"What's the matter? Why are you looking at me like that, Sam?" I asked, alarmed.

"Keep very still, Riley," he whispered. "Gabbra's in flight. I think she will live."

A large Swallow-tail butterfly landed on my shoulder. We watched, fascinated, as it fluttered above Sam's head, brushed his cheek with its wings and settled on the door of Gabbra's hut.

I put my hand out slowly. The butterfly landed briefly on my finger, then it seemed to vanish.

"I knew Gabbra would send me a sign!" I said out loud, shivers tingling up my spine.

"Me too," whispered Sam.

He taught the women how to observe Gabbra's condition, and showed them how to fill the rubber bag with water so she would not get dehydrated.

"Riley, as a last resort, I must prepare for a dangerous mission tonight. It'll take me seven hours or more, but I must drive immediately to Somalia and hope to be back before nightfall tomorrow. Pray for Gabbra." And he was gone.

I found Nagya sitting on a rock just outside the *manyatta*. Out of respect for Gabbra, he wore a black ceremonial *shuka* over one shoulder. Without speaking, he held my hand, turning it over and caressing my palm.

"Riley, you are very special to me," he said, looking seriously into my eyes. I was so angry about his behaviour with Ayasha that I didn't want to believe him. Perhaps it was from all the uncertainty about her relationship with him and my shock of seeing Gabbra in a coma. He had comforted Ayasha when she howled over Gabbra's limp body, cradled her so tenderly in his arms, and even looked at her the same way he had gazed at *me*. And I felt ignored.

My secret feelings of adoration for this apparently uninterested Borana warrior enraged me. Tears of frustration welled up inside and I dragged my hand away angrily.

"You're a very cruel man, Nagya. Why do you tease me? I've had enough!" I hissed.

Nagya looked astonished. "What is the reason for this unexpected explosion, Riley?" he said, looking hurt.

Then I turned on him. "Stop pretending, Nagya. I've tried to ask what Ayasha meant to you, but you always changed the subject. Even

Gabbra doesn't have the courage to tell me."

Nagya stood up, towering over me, frowning. "Why are you so angry? What are you talking about?" Then he laughed so hard he sat down again. "Now I see what you've been thinking all this time," he said, grinning. "Come here, Riley-girl. I will tell you everything."

"I don't want to hear it!" I snapped, cupping my hands over my ears.

He pulled my hands down gently and sat me on his knee. Then I clenched my knuckles into fists until they turned white to try and stop the tears from falling. I was not going to let him see how I felt. As soon as he tilted my face toward his, I knew it was too late. Flinging my arms around him, I sobbed into his chest like I did with my father when I was small and upset.

"Ayasha is my cousin," he said flatly. "I love her like a sister. Even though she tried to poison Gabbra, she did what she thought was her duty."

In shock, I stood up quickly, stunned into silence, not able to comprehend what he said. My legs felt weak and I touched the rock to steady myself.

I blinked at Nagya in disbelief. "Ayasha tried to kill my best friend? Why, Nagya? Why? Where is she? I want to tear her apart. ...And what's with this 'duty' thing?"

Nagya grabbed me and sat me down, then opened his mouth to speak, when I interrupted him. I hardly recognized my own husky voice. "Ayasha is your *cousin*?"

"I thought you knew. Didn't Gabbra tell you?" he said.

I remembered Nagya and Ayasha dancing together, her coolness toward me, always checking me out, Nagya's tender caring for her. Then she poisoned her own cousin out of duty. It didn't add up.

"You mean...you're not in love with Ayasha?" I stammered.

Nagya looked at me from under his thick black eyelashes, an amused smile on his face. "I'm shocked that you could even *think* of such an impossible relationship. Riley, you must understand that cousins protect one another in our culture. My mother and Ayasha's mother were sisters. They were both taken by the Somali bandits," said Nagya.

I stared at him, paralysed. I remembered the Chief telling me about the *Shifta* attack, but I didn't realize Ayasha and Nagya were related.

"Ayasha tried to cling to her mother's hand, but she was beaten over the head with a *simi*," continued Nagya. "She ran, bleeding, to a thorn tree and climbed to the topmost branch. My father found her naked and in shock three days later. Since then she has not spoken one word until now. I think she's unbalanced at the moment, but she took on the silent role of watching over Gabbra and me. Only one week before that fateful day, the two girls had taken the oath together with their mothers to keep the Borana tradition—or die if they broke the promise."

I listened in silence while Nagya continued. "I went to see Kallu, the spiritual Head Elder, to look for answers. I knew my sister had gone to talk to him. He told me he had listened carefully to Gabbra's reasons for change, and how she confessed she had broken the oath to her mother. After she left, he sent one of the Elders to bring my cousin Ayasha to him for a private meeting."

"But wait a minute," I interrupted him again, eventually finding my voice. "Are you really saying that Ayasha poisoned her own cousin?"

"I haven't finished yet," said Nagya. "Kallu commanded Ayasha to kill Gabbra by traditional poisoning—a warning to other girls that breaking a serious promise was a death sentence. In Kallu and the Elders' presence, Ayasha took the silent oath to kill the one she loved most."

Nagya gently pushed the hair away from my face. "Now that Ayasha has calmed down— surprising herself with the return of her voice— she has told me that because she made a promise to her mother, she was forced to obey Kallu," he said. "She took the snuff box from Kallu's hut and walked over to the camel pen. She poured the crystallized snake venom into a *gourd*, filled it with milk and persuaded Gabbra—using hand signals—to ride with her to the well for water. When they got there, Ayasha offered her cousin the *gourd* of camel's milk and poison mixture, but she forgot to shake the potion. Just as Gabbra was sipping the refreshment, a flock of doves flew up unexpectedly from the well and alarmed her. She dropped the *gourd* and spilled most of the poison that had settled at the bottom. I don't know how much venom Gabbra got, but even a tiny drop of ingested neurotoxin is dangerous.

"Gabbra clutched at her chest, probably because she had trouble breathing, then called out for help, slurring her words. She swayed, trying to grab the side of the trough, and fell to the ground. Ayasha was told that hungry hyenas would feed on Gabbra's body before nightfall, leaving no trace behind.

My throat began to gag but Nagya continued.

"Ayasha got back on her camel and went directly to the Elders via another route. Her arrival alone was confirmation of Gabbra's apparent death."

"And how did Jillo know what Ayasha had done?" I asked, having overcome my feeling of nausea.

"When you brought Jillo to me, he told me that he had seen Ayasha entering the Elders' hut. He waited outside and when she came out carrying a small snuff container, he followed her to the camel pen and watched her empty the contents into a *gourd* and fill it with milk. Even children know what is inside Kallu's special snuff box. Ayasha and Gabbra mounted one of the camels and took off toward the well. He didn't have to tell me any more—I knew."

I sat close beside Nagya, trying to understand all the recent happenings.

"I found Gabbra on the ground beside the well. I knew she had been poisoned because she arched her back in convulsions and foamed at the mouth before losing consciousness. She must have swallowed just enough to put her into a coma," he continued.

"Believing Gabbra to be dead and eaten by hyenas, Ayasha was paralysed when she saw me bringing my sister's limp body back to the *manyatta*. The shock of seeing Gabbra and the realization of what she had just done to the one she loved most must have brought back her voice," said Nagya.

"What will Ayasha do now that she can speak? Is she an outcast because she tried to kill Gabbra?"

"Although Ayasha attempted murder, her job is done and she is in no trouble," said Nagya. "Rules of the Borana culture, set by the Elders, have been carried out."

"Then who sabotaged the pipeline?" I asked

Nagya, intrigued.

"My cousin."

"Ayasha?" I whispered, horrified.

I blinked rapidly, trying to think back to my sleepless night in the tent. I recalled the tremor of someone running softly past my tent in the early hours of the morning, and the distant sound of glass being broken down at the well.

"She had no fear," continued Nagya. "She watched me handle all kinds of reptiles when she was a little girl. Kallu—the one who must be obeyed—said the spirits would tell her what to do, but he knew that chameleons and carpet vipers would be evidence of witchcraft to the Kenyan crew members, and they would stop building the pipeline. Without our intervention, Mathenge and his pals would have gone home while the equipment would lie useless and rusting for a hundred years."

"But why *her*, and not someone else?" I began.

Nagya looked down at his feet. "I figured it out. Although that poor girl has been on an emotional rollercoaster, she does not recognize remorse or guilt. When the Elders heard that the pipeline installation was going ahead without their consent, they were dismayed. Because Ayasha was not capable of divulging secret plans, Kallu summoned her to his hut, where she was first given orders by the Elders to sabotage the pipeline because they believed it would interfere with Borana tradition. It was also to avenge Gabbra's confession of breaking the oath she made to her mother and falling in love with a man from another tribe. Ayasha was forced to carry out her own promise to kill the person she loved most in the only non-painful way she knew."

"Have the Elders called a halt to sabotage?" I asked.

"My young journalist always has questions!" said Nagya. "Because Ayasha is finally able to converse with the Elders, they have confirmed that her responsibility has now been fulfilled. After hours of discussion, my father and I think we have convinced Kallu that in order for the Borana tribe to survive, the pipeline has to be accepted. He understands there will be great change in lifestyle, but at the same time the culture must be kept alive through music, traditional stories and dance."

I tried to unravel the ropes of my tangled thoughts. Although I distrusted Ayasha from the start, Nagya's explanation was so clear that I found myself erasing all vivid memories that hurt me. I felt ashamed of myself for thinking so badly about her.

As if he heard what I was thinking, Nagya said, "Ayasha will be very happy to become a teacher of our traditions and customs now that she can talk. You know, the only time I ever saw my cousin smile was when I danced with her. You disappeared just when I was going to choose you."

"Choose me for what?" I asked, snapping my head up quickly. Irish pixies skipped happy jigs on my once-uncertain thoughts.

"For my dancing partner, of course!" said Nagya.

Exhausted from the day's calamity, I returned to my hut and slept until noon the next day. Sam's LandRover pulled into the *manyatta* but I was so emotionally drained, I didn't talk to anyone. I lay on my camel skin for hours, trying to figure out what I was going to do back home without Gabbra.

I heard singing and my heart forgot to beat for a moment. Was it my imagination or did I really hear Gabbra's song? I listened for a few minutes, trying to figure out what was happening. It was *not* a dream—she *was* singing.

Bursting through her doorway, I called out, "Gabbra, is that you? You're awake!" In the subdued light I saw Sam, Ayasha and two strange women standing beside Gabbra's bed.

Gabbra sat up and held out her arms to me. I ran to her and buried my head in her hair and cried.

"I have much to tell you, my sweet friend,"

said Gabbra. "I think I've been on a journey to the heavens, but returned to earth. Apparently it was not yet my time."

"Gabbra, who are these people?" I pointed to the women dressed in dirty white robes. They were thin but strikingly beautiful, with high cheekbones similar to Gabbra. Their heads were covered in soft cream-coloured gossamer shawls edged with ornate embroidery—typical of Somalia. I noticed, with surprise, that Chief Jallaba had his arm around the shoulders of one of the women.

"It was not *me* singing, Riley," said Gabbra. "This is my mother. Sam has risked his life by travelling into Somalia through dangerous *Shifta* territory to find the one person who might be able to revive me."

"I have nothing to say about my fellow Somalis," muttered Sam, in a shaky voice. He had spots of blood on the front of his shirt, cuts on his cheek and a large bandage around his head.

I opened my mouth to ask questions, but Sam tiptoed weakly out of the hut and joined Nagya. Gabbra continued. "Sam took containers of water, four bleating fat-tailed sheep, and a supply of camel meat. The fact that he spoke to them in their own language, and offered to treat the sick and seriously wounded bandits, may have swayed the men into reluctantly trading two of their wives: Ayasha's mother and mine. The trade was completed on condition Sam take an oath that he return with medical supplies. Even so, they beat him badly and the LandRover is peppered with bullet holes."

"So it wasn't *you* singing?" I repeated.

"My mother sang the song she taught me when I was a child. Sam believes that perhaps it was the familiar voice and her appearance that brought me out of my coma," explained Gabbra.

Wiping the tears gently from my astonished face, Gabbra said, "Riley, I want to introduce you to my mother." She spoke in *Galla* language to the woman standing beside her father. Gabbra's mother moved toward me. Smiling, she held both my hands in hers and, with head bowed, spoke softly.

Gabbra laughed. "She is saying you are a special gift sent from Heaven. She worships the beautiful white-girl-with-small-breasts!" I grinned at Gabbra for her comical interpretation, but smiled politely at her mother.

"It is time," said Nagya, interrupting us. He took his mother by the arm. "Riley, we are going to have an important meeting with Kallu and the Elders to welcome our mothers home. I don't think my mother will speak to me of prison life in Somalia so I may never know what happened, but that is the past. Now we will celebrate their return, and their future. By the way, Jillo wants to play *mbau* with you outside. I tried to persuade him to let you win this time."

Throwing me his typical playful grin, he led the two mothers and his father out of the hut.

Herding boys on the job.
(pic: Margaret Hayes)

Chapter 15

JILLO AND THE BEANSTALK

SUMMER VACATION WAS COMING TO AN END and I dreaded the thought of returning home to Canada in three days. Funny how I've changed, I thought, smiling to myself. I remembered there was a time just a few months ago when I was so spoiled and angry that I couldn't *wait* to leave Dumbuluk, simply because I thought Nagya was avoiding me.

Jillo jumped up quickly from the *mbau* game

we were playing in the sand and pointed at a tiny
cloud of dust in the distance, swirling our way. It
was Nagya. He had promised to take a break from
the pipeline.

"Finish the game, Borana Boy," I said.
"Nagya won't be here for another ten minutes."
With nifty fingers, Jillo scooped up all my camel
pebbles, herding them into his own corral and
beat me, once again. Jillo challenged me for two
days but I still sucked at this game!

A truck roared noisily into the *manyatta*, with
the Kikuyu workers laughing and waving at me
from the front cab.

Nagya leapt out, shouting excitedly, "Jump
in, you two! We've got something to show you.
Riley, bring your camera and journal."

Nagya let down the tailgate and hauled Jillo
and me into the empty truck, motioning us to sit
further up with our backs to the driver's cab.

"Make room for me," said Nagya, wiggling
between us. "Mathenge said we should come and
get you. He wants to show you how far we've
progressed." He banged his palm twice on the
back window, making a circling motion with his
finger. I supposed that was an indication for
Mathenge to drive back to the well.

"Another load of pipes has arrived from
Nairobi, and one more shipment is coming next
week," Nagya yelled above the rumbling noise of
our truck.

"Tell me more when we get there," I shouted. "We're swallowing too much dust!"

After a while, Nagya nudged me and pointed to a clump of Acacia trees. "That's the proposed site for our new village," he yelled. "We'll have lots of shade for the cattle. Look, see how far we've got with the pipeline." Nagya and the crew had progressed faster than I believed possible.

I nodded and smiled at him. I joked out loud that if *happiness* meant sitting in the back of a rumbling truck with two of my best talkative friends and sand filling our mouths, then life was good.

We continued on to the well, and laughed when Jillo tried to stand up in the truck as it bounced over rocks and deep pot-holes.

"This is it! This is the magic place Jillo wants to show you," said Nagya, pulling Jillo down beside him before he fell over.

Bang! went Nagya's hand on the cab roof. Mathenge stopped the truck, let down the tail-gate and helped us out. Jillo ran helter-skelter down to the well. A familiar perfumed sweetness wafted past my nose as I tried to keep up with him. He plunged his sticky hand into mine and pulled me to a patch of ground hidden by a hedge of thorns. I lifted my head to sniff the air and stared in amazement.

Peeping from beneath a mass of creeping vines and tendrils, twelve large melons lay ripening in the sun. Looking from Jillo to Nagya, it slowly dawned on me. When I had visited the well for the first time, I'd been carrying around a melon in my backpack. I remembered sharing the fruit with Jillo and watched him stuff the disgusting, slimy seeds into his shirt pocket.

"How did he know what to do?" I asked Nagya.

"Remember that kids' picture book he was always looking at?" said Nagya.

I nodded. *Jack and the Beanstalk*—the old classic tale.

"I won the book when I was a student at the Catholic Mission, and gave it to Jillo years ago," said Nagya. "Although he cannot read, he studied the pictures of Jack throwing magic beans into the earth. I was puzzled at first, until I realized what he was doing. Jillo said he was really disappointed *his* plants did not reach the sky like *Jack's* did."

We watched Jillo carrying a *gourd* of water to his secret garden.

"Every time he travelled to the well, he would water the seeds until they had germinated and sprung into life," said Nagya. "This plant originated in Africa centuries ago. It needs the right amount of water, sunshine and dryness, and we have found that we have the perfect growing conditions right here."

"I'm impressed," I said.

"With proper irrigation, this melon farm

could be a valuable money-making venture," said Nagya. "We'll buy a refrigerated truck to transport the fruit to Nairobi. Now how's *that* for a change in Jillo's lifestyle, Riley?"

"Better than herding camels all day," I replied with a grin.

A loud honking noise startled us. Bumbling along the track was a bright yellow bus and, from out of the window, appeared a very dark-skinned hand, waving madly at us.

"Sam!" I shouted, recognising him. "Where on earth did you get that monster?"

He pointed to the printing on one side of the bus.

DONATED TO THE GIRLS AND BOYS OF DUMBULUK

—from the students & teachers of West End High Private School—

VANCOUVER, BRITISH COLUMBIA, CANADA

"I phoned your school and told the Board members about the damaged pipeline equipment and that Gabbra had survived a devastating illness. They agreed, unanimously, to grant a large sum of money for a school bus and replacement of the solar panel system," Sam explained. "They said she sets an example to students through her dedication to music, high standard of academics and strong desire to enter the field of medicine."

Sam picked up the bus in Nairobi and drove through the night so he could get to Dumbuluk before I returned to Canada. "I have to get some sleep at the *manyatta* and I must tend to Gabbra. See you later," he yelled, as he revved the engine, shifted gears and headed back down the track, leaving us cloaked in dust.

It dawned on me that Gabbra had touched every person who mattered in her life.

Back at the *manyatta,* Nagya sat quietly beside me, watching as I wrote in my journal for the day.

Eventually he spoke. "I have some exciting news, Riley-girl. Father and I have been talking to the Elders, and they are now confident that the tribe can be persuaded to become farmers."

"That's a huge change for them, Nagya," I said.

"They have no choice," he said. "The land has been reduced to desert because of the drought. Even when the rains come, it will take months for vegetation to grow back. But, since Gabbra's revival and the return of both mothers, community esteem has risen," he continued. "The Elders believe that Gabbra is all-powerful. She is forgiven for breaking her oath and she is now not in any danger of further plots against her life. My father and I have persuaded Kallu and the Elders that Gabbra must do what she has set her heart on: to study medicine in Canada and return to Africa as a flying doctor. And when the Elders select the next Chief of Dumbuluk, who knows, perhaps Jillo will be the right choice!" he said, laughing.

"And what of Ayasha, now that her voice has returned?" I asked.

"There will be no more sabotage of irrigation equipment. She will continue the Borana culture through song and traditional stories, coached by the two mothers and the other women in the tribe."

"So what's your strategy now, Nagya?" I asked, eagerly, hoping he would include me in his plans.

"Two large water tanks and building supplies for a permanent community village are on the way to the new site, and a replacement solar pump has just arrived," Nagya said.

I flung my arms impulsively around his neck. "That pipeline is a hungry iron snake with a solar-heated heart!"

Nagya hugged me and laughed. "You're never at a loss for words, Riley. You've created a breathing metal monster."

"And now what will happen?" I asked, expectantly.

"Okay, I'll tell you. Half our camels will be

sold to buy cattle and seed. Fields for pasture and melons will be reclaimed when we set up irrigation. We'll take your idea, Riley, and copy the Canadian ranchers by using moveable irrigation equipment on wheels, with water coming directly from the second water tank," he said.

"And after that, Nagya? What about life after melons and irrigation?"

Nagya thought for a moment and continued. "I'm happy with the school bus now that we have a driver from the mission coming to help us," said Nagya. "The mission Fathers are building dormitories so that both boys *and* girls can stay in town at school for five days a week in exchange for supplies of water and camel milk."

I couldn't believe he was dodging my obvious probing. "What about *your* future, Nagya," I blurted out.

Nagya looked composed and confident as he explained. "My father has convinced my mother that both Gabbra and I are too westernized to be expected to live here and that we now have our own future agendas. Gabbra has been given permission to return to Vancouver with Sam when she completely recovers, and there is money set aside for her to study medicine when she graduates from high school."

I began to feel uneasy. Did I come into *any* of his personal future plans at all? I narrowed my eyes at him, beginning to feel annoyed.

Nagya frowned and gave me a questioning look. Why couldn't I tell him? I was notorious for being outspoken, and he knew I wasn't afraid of delivering a lengthy speech, but now I was tongue-tied. I found myself panicking. I could not even find the words I'd been longing to tell him, until they came out all garbled.

"I don't get it, Nagya," I said, stamping my foot angrily. "Is this the end of our relationship, or are you deliberately avoiding a commitment?" I raged at him.

Nagya grinned in such a way that I felt he was crawling around inside my mind, tugging on yarns of emotions and mixing them all up.

"If it's my personal feelings you're insisting on asking about, Riley-girl, I'm like Jack climbing the beanstalk—my dreams are also seen from high places!"

That tantalizing comment left me feeling completely baffled and frustrated. I feared that although Nagya had definite ideas for the future, I may not be part of them. I knew he had feelings for me, so why was he still carrying this teasing evasiveness to the edge? Our bitter-sweet relationship seemed on the brink of something weird yet wonderful. I'd either plummet to the depths of despair, or soar like a bird on a thermal of passion.

A tribal Elder. Men wearing *shukas*. Pics: Margaret Hayes

Chapter 16

A WARM WIND OF CHANGE

BEFORE NAGYA LEFT FOR NAIROBI to
pick up more parts for the pipeline, Dad radio-
called the Chief with the request to drive Gabbra,
me and our backpacks to the airstrip later that
day.

Since Nagya and I had not spoken to one
another since my outburst, I went to spend some
'thinking time' on his special observation rock,
just outside the *manyatta*.

Looking out across the dry plain, I tried not to dwell on the probability that I wouldn't see Nagya before we left Dumbuluk. Ashamed after lashing out so desperately at him, I wanted a sandstorm to whisk my regrettable words far away into the distance.

Further down the track from where I was sitting, some rude horn-blaring broke my train of thought, and a truck stopped with a sharp screech, covering me in dust.

Nagya leaned out of the truck window. "See what I have for the well," he said, "I wanted you to see it before you left for home." I beamed happily at him. Nagya jumped out and lifted down the tailgate, pulling a large bronze plaque from the back.

DUMBULUK
Solar Pump & Pipeline

Sponsored by:
International Development & Disaster Agency
Government of Kenya

Concept and Fundraising:
Riley Forbes

It took me a while to read the words. "Wow!" I said, as he put the heavy plaque back in the truck. "It's beautiful, Nagya."

"Come and sit on the tailgate with me," he said, patting a space beside him. "By the way, your father left a message that he'd be delayed for a couple of hours."

Nagya pointed to something in the distance. "Look, jackals running after an old, weak-looking gazelle."

"Now I see them," I said, excitedly, adjusting my camera's telephoto lens. A family of four black-backed jackals fanned out as they sprinted after their prey, yipping and squealing as they closed in on the kill.

"Reminds me of those lovely girls on the steps at your school when I came to visit you after I graduated from flying school. Perhaps I was the prey?" laughed Nagya.

Piqued with his chauvinism, I glared at him and refused to answer.

"I have something else for you," he said, with an amused look on his face. Nagya took from his pocket a necklace that had a little pouch attached to it. He whipped off the baseball cap I was wearing, pushed my braids over to one side and tied the necklace around my neck.

Feeling my cheeks flush, I looked down at the leather pouch settling on my chest and opened the flap. My fingers searched nervously for whatever was inside. In my palm lay a smelly clay camel—'*Ata Allah*'—with a miniature red scarf tied around its neck—just like the original one he had given me that broke when I fell down the well.

"You made me another *God's Gift*," I said, smiling.

"Actually I didn't make the *first* one, and I didn't make this one either," he said. "I got Ayasha to do it. Boys don't make toys. It's not a guy thing."

I looked up quickly, not because of Nagya's remarks, but from an unusual gust of wind and the deep rolling sound of thunder, like faraway drums announcing an important event.

We stopped talking and stared at something moving beside us. Perched on the rock was a red-headed male Agama lizard—the colour of screaming scarlet from his armpits to his nose. The rest of his scaly body, legs and tail were covered in a beautiful turquoise and shimmering purple. This miniature dragon stared at us with his beady eyes while he did a few push-ups with his forearms, then wriggled away.

I told Nagya that his sister liked the Agama lizard because of the creature's independence, strength and intelligence.

"Riley, that's the sign I've been looking for. Perhaps the lizard is telling me something," whispered Nagya.

We both stood very still, not wishing to move.

"Tell me what you like best about this Borana man called *Nagya*, standing here beside you," he said, with a serious face.

"First, let me tell you why I *don't* want to live here," I began, talking quickly. "I fear the *Shifta* attacks. I cannot survive on a diet of milk and blood, or wash my body in camel's urine, or travel around like a nomad."

I was trying to say that I never wanted to let him go, but where would our rough paths of destiny lead us?

"And what do you think of *me*, Nagya?" I asked.

"You are avoiding my question, and I did not *expect* you to live here," he said, solemnly. "I see what is missing in a Borana woman. The first time I met you I was an arrogant camel-herder and you were a pesky thirteen-year-old, but I dreamed of you for three years. I'm attracted to your personality and sense of humour. I find you intellectually challenging…"

I missed a chunk of his profound statement as my agile mind stumbled to an intoxicating height.

"…could be a team," he was saying. "I'll pilot doctors to tribes needing medical assistance, and you become the photo-journalist you're destined to be. Together we'll make the world aware of the vanishing cultures and tribes of Africa."

My heart fluttered rapidly like the wings of a Swallow-tail butterfly. Nagya had never admitted his private inner feelings to me.

Before I could comment, he went on, "I also like your wild impulsiveness, your infectious laughter and tears, and especially your enthusiasm. I'm very proud of you, Riley-girl. You never cease to surprise me," he said softly, cupping his hands around my face.

"Through your efforts you have made a difference in the survival of my people, and I won't ever forget that. I admire your determination to improve life for the Borana tribe, but I think you know I also cannot live here in Dumbuluk. I cannot reverse the fact that I'm too westernized," he admitted.

I took a deep breath. There was something I had wanted to ask Nagya for a long time.

"Nagya, did you resuscitate me when I fell down the well?"

"Yes," he answered, with a smirk on his face.

I looked down at my feet.

"Yes, I did," he said again, his eyes twinkling. "But your lips were ice-cold then." I think he enjoyed watching me squirm.

"I have more gifts for you, Riley. I made them myself." He dropped a small pair of black sandals onto the ground beside me—shoes similar to the ones he was wearing.

"They're high-fashion Borana re-treads," he quipped.

"Yeah, *right!*" I snorted, curling the corner of my lip at his sarcasm.

"Here, sit down and try them on. I guarantee you'll run faster in these," he said, guiding me by the hand to a smooth rock. Nagya pulled off my sneakers and wedged my feet firmly into the rubber tire sandals. He adjusted the criss-cross inner tire strips over my toes and snapped the band around my heels.

"Comfortable?" he queried.

"Fantastic!" I answered.

He then reached over and dragged something else from the back of the truck. "Ayasha sent you this," he said, handing me a long leather strap covered in an intricate blue design, with white beads stitched along the neckpiece.

"I remember," I said. "It's the strap that fits around the neck of a newly-married woman to stop her from being too frisky."

"See how it fits, Borana-girl," Nagya said, jumping down from the tailgate.

"Why don't I put it on *you*, Nagya?" I said, also stepping down from the back of the truck. "After all, it was you who said that changes in tradition were inevitable."

Without a word, he turned around while I

tied the leather strap around his neck.

"Can't a girl tame her new boyfriend?" I teased.

"Only if she can catch him," said Nagya, darting away from me. He bounded like a young colt over dust-coated bushes, the leather strap dangling down his back. When I finally caught up to him, he scooped me up and held me tightly in his arms.

"It's about time I had a *warm* kiss from you, my white Borana-girl," he said, kissing me passionately, while my confined heart leapt free from its cage.

"I have to take you back to the *manyatta* now," he murmured, "and maybe you can bring us some refreshment by milking Gabbra's camel before we have to leave for the airstrip."

This time, I didn't need a second invitation to milk that pesky beast.

Bruised-looking clouds stumbled aimlessly in a sky of dark indigo blue. Dead leaves rustled in an Acacia tree and long yellow grass flattened with the impact of a strong gust of wind. I heard more thunder rumbling in the distance and a large teardrop of rain exploded like a miniature bomb onto the dry parched earth beside us, sending up a spray of fine dust particles.

"Gabbra was right," Nagya said quietly, his fingers interlacing mine. "She told us that sometimes tragedy strikes after a severe drought, and then the first drops of rain fall. It's the Borana sign of *good luck*."

I also remembered her saying those words.

I shivered slightly as a warm wind danced across my shoulders. With eyes closed, I tilted my head upward as more drops of rain stung my cheeks and splattered onto my rubber tire sandals.

At last, I could feel a definite change in the air. Not only did the change signify survival of the Borana tribe, but the potential of a future for us.

Nagya, the warrior, and I—his white Borana-girl—were destined to be together.

Glossary of Swahili Words

Word	Pronunciation	Definition
ata Allah	ah-tah Ah-lah:	God's gift
bwana	bwah-nah	Mr./Mister
gourd	gohrd	round or sausage-shaped wooden container for holding liquid
jambo	jahm-boh	greetings, hello
jiko	jee-koh	small portable cooking stove with hot coals below
kanga or kikoi	kahng-gah or kee-koi	woman's cloth sarong usually folded securely above the breast.
kibuyu	kee-boo-yoo	water pot made of palm fronds, dried mud and dung
kinyonga	kee-nyong-gah	chameleon
mbau	um-bah-oo	Maasai wooden board game using small, hard seeds or pebbles (this game is also used by many other tribes, often gouged out of rock)
manyatta	mahn-yah-tah	huts and livestock enclosed by protective thorn bushes
Ngai	ung-eye-ee	God
nyoka	nyoh-kah	snake
posho	poh-shoh	ground white maize-meal boiled in water to form sticky porridge
safari	sah-fah-ree	journey
salaams	sah-laahms	blessings/greetings/peace
Shifta	Sheef-tah	bandits, terrorists
shitani	shee-tah-nee	devil

shuka	shooh-kah	man's cotton cloth worn over one shoulder
simi	see-mee	very sharp, long, two-edged knife
tutaonana	too-tah-oh-nah-nah	Kikuyu language meaning 'we shall meet again'

ISBN 142510500-9